One Day the Shadow Passed

One Day the Shadow Passed

Jonathan Reggio

HAY HOUSE

Australia • Canada • Hong Kong • India
South Africa • United Kingdom • United States

First published and distributed in the United Kingdom by:
Hay House UK Ltd, 292B Kensal Rd, London W10 5BE. Tel.: (44) 20 8962 1230;
Fax: (44) 20 8962 1239. www.hayhouse.co.uk

Published and distributed in the United States of America by:
Hay House, Inc., PO Box 5100, Carlsbad, CA 92018-5100. Tel.: (1) 760 431 7695 or
(800) 654 5126; Fax: (1) 760 431 6948 or (800) 650 5115. www.hayhouse.com

Published and distributed in Australia by:
Hay House Australia Ltd, 18/36 Ralph St, Alexandria NSW 2015.
Tel.: (61) 2 9669 4299; Fax: (61) 2 9669 4144. www.hayhouse.com.au

Published and distributed in the Republic of South Africa by:
Hay House SA (Pty), Ltd, PO Box 990, Witkoppen 2068. Tel./Fax: (27) 11 467 8904.
www.hayhouse.co.za

Published and distributed in India by:
Hay House Publishers India, Muskaan Complex, Plot No.3, B-2, Vasant Kunj, New
Delhi – 110 070. Tel.: (91) 11 4176 1620; Fax: (91) 11 4176 1630. www.hayhouse.co.in

Distributed in Canada by:
Raincoast, 9050 Shaughnessy St, Vancouver, BC V6P 6E5. Tel.: (1) 604 323 7100;
Fax: (1) 604 323 2600

A catalogue record for this book is available from the British Library.

ISBN 978-1-84850-847-7

Printed and bound in Great Britain by TJ International, Padstow, Cornwall.

For Will and Ali

THE SUN

Many years ago I went on a long walk down a path unknown to travellers in that very old region of Japan called Shikoku Island.

It is hard to imagine it today, but at the time when I undertook my journey the countryside was made up of thousands upon thousands of smallholdings that were still being farmed in exactly the same manner as they had been farmed in the days of the samurai. The great Japanese automobile and electronics firms had yet to dominate the world; most people still lived and worked on the land pursuing lives little different from those of their ancestors, and on Shikoku Island itself many of the farmers still went out into the paddy fields dressed in the traditional clothes of the Japanese peasant.

The island is divided down the middle by a chain of mountains. To the east lie rich alluvial plains where rice and barley and other winter grains are grown. To the west the mountains descend into gentle hills and eventually peter out into the quiet waters of the Inland Sea. Orchards of citrus and persimmons and chestnuts and pomegranates cover these wooded slopes and below, down on the plains, vast networks of paddy fields and irrigation channels stretch away towards the horizon. The entire island has been cultivated for millennia with an intensity that is seen nowhere else in Japan.

The path I had chosen to follow all those years ago was an ancient pilgrims' route that has been trodden for centuries by the men and women of Japan. The pilgrimage begins at Mount Koya in Wakayama Prefecture and ends at the village of Karamachi, nestled on the shores of the Inland Sea. The journey takes forty days and forty nights, which is long enough to ensure that the solitary wayfarer has plenty of time to think – long enough indeed to ensure that he or she stops thinking altogether and begins simply to exist. For only once the mind is stopped, say the Zen monks, can it be truly repaired.

The path passes through some of the most sublime countryside in Japan. Along the way it is dotted with roadside temples, built long centuries ago to offer food and shelter to the weary pilgrims. In the evening, among the silent stone walls of these ancient temples, the pilgrims share the spartan but healthy hospitality of the Buddhist monks. These holy men sleep on stone pillows, they rise at dawn, they eat gruel or boiled rice garnished with a handful of fresh herbs, then they put on their sedge hats and take up their staffs, and their voyage into the interior begins again.

Ever since I was a boy I had longed to make the journey to Japan and walk the pilgrims' route, but life has a way of continuously throwing up obstacles – good and bad – which prevent us from achieving even our most modest ambitions.

I was seven years old when I first discovered a small book on Japan in my local library; from that day on, my fascination with the country and its people began to grow. Its art and poetry and history spoke to me like nothing else, and by the time I left school I knew hundreds of haikus by heart. I knew the name of every river and every town in the Archipelago, and the epic tales of the great samurai were as familiar to me as the stories of the Kings and Queens of England.

But the years passed and there was always some reason why I was obliged to remain at home: a lack of money, the need to work, my commitments to my family. Such ordinary things prevented me from pursuing my dreams but finally, one day, I found myself at the end of a long summer. I was without a job and had no immediate prospect of getting one. I had time to spare and for once I even had enough money in my pocket to afford the ticket to Japan. I longed to breathe fresh mountain air and feel foreign soil under my feet. In any case, I couldn't think what else to do with my life. All I knew was that I wasn't ready to throw in my lot with one particular career.

This sense of indecision was partly just a factor of my youth, but there was something deeper, too: my vague awareness that the world was heading in the wrong direction. Everywhere I looked the news was bad. Forests were being chopped down, coral reefs were being destroyed, indigenous cultures were collapsing under the pressures of Westernization – and yet there was no evidence that the world was becoming a safer or happier place.

I feared indeed that the opposite might be true. The environment was being degraded, the rich of the world were becoming richer whilst the poor, who in the past had at least lived sustainable lives and had pride in their own cultures, were now being dragged into dependency on this global machine. Nature was misunderstood on a fundamental level, for even the most well-intentioned programmes of development seemed always to produce unforeseen side-effects, and every benefit delivered by progress carried within itself the seed of some future disaster.

And the myriad processes that were driving this change were so complicated that they seemed to be utterly beyond the grasp of a normal person's comprehension. I felt confused and I did not know how to understand this changing world, nor indeed what my role in it was supposed to be.

With these anxieties weighing heavily on my mind, I set off for Japan. I had no real preconceptions about what I might discover there. I packed a guidebook, a well-thumbed copy of Matsuo Basho's haikus and a couple of changes of clothes. I hoped to live off rice and vegetables and to keep out of the big cities, where my meagre funds would soon be exhausted. I had done little planning other than choosing the route. I was giving myself up to destiny and I was launching myself into the timeless dreamland of rural Japan and tempting fate to show me a new path.

As I was soon to find out, fate needs little encouragement, and my life was about to be changed for ever.

On the seventh day of the pilgrimage I found myself wading through a vast expanse of waist-high grass that marked the boundary between the rice-growing plains of the east and the wooded slopes at the south-western end of the island.

I was still in the state of euphoria that had overcome me as soon as I had stepped off the aeroplane. After all these years my dreams had finally come true: I was in Japan, walking the pilgrims' route. It was a heart-achingly beautiful September day and there was not a cloud in the sky. So bright and strong was the sunshine in fact that, even though the brim of my traditional white-sedge pilgrim's hat shaded my eyes, I was forced to squint at the view.

On the horizon to the north I could see the majestic mountains of the central highlands and before me, tantalizingly close now, were the shady wooded slopes of the first foothills. Only the noise of my legs swishing through the tall grass seemed to mark my progress. At one point I turned to look back over my tracks; a long thin shadowy line disappeared off towards the horizon and was lost in the golden haze of grass and the last, now distant, rice farms. With every step that I took I was heading further and further into the most remote and unpopulated countryside of Japan, and as I did so a profound sense of elation – a sense of elation that I hadn't felt in years – began to rise within me.

Before I had left home I had dug out an old history of Shikoku Island from my local library. It said that this had once been one of the richest areas of Japan before agriculture was overtaken by technology and industry. Great dynasties had sprung up and perished here among the lush rice paddies of the alluvial plains, and even today the fields of Ehime Prefecture over which I was now treading still produced the highest rice yields in all the land.

I watched as a gentle breeze caused a shiver to cross the measureless sea of grass, and I was reminded of a haiku by Basho whose poetry was never far from my mind throughout the duration of my walk.

The waving of the summer grass
Is all that remains
Of the dreams and ambitions
Of long-buried warriors.

Full of wonder, I pushed on up the rolling grasslands half expecting to kick an ancient leather helmet or tread upon a rusty sword.

By sunset I had reached my home for the night, a derelict Buddhist temple that was to be my last refuge down on the plains. The guardian of the place, an ancient monk, cooked brown rice that he scooped from a sack slumped against the stone altar. I drew water for the meal, crystal clear and sweet as wine, from the still-functioning well that stood in the centre of the temple yard, surrounded on all sides by crumbling walls. We ate the gruel in silence and then we curled up to sleep side by side on the temple floor.

It had been a good day. The walking had been hard, but the countryside was so beautiful, so tranquil, that it was impossible not to feel uplifted, not to feel, even, a sense of tentative optimism.

As the night drew on and I lay there unable to sleep the wind got up and began to howl. It was a dry, parched summer storm and as I tossed and turned on the hard, cold floor listening to the moan and screech of the trees, I found myself thinking about the people I had passed today working in the fields, about how very different our lives were nowadays in the great cities of the world, how complicated things were today and how the world seemed to be hurtling in the wrong direction.

Eventually, I managed to drop off and grab a few hours of fitful sleep. When dawn came I wasted no time in gathering up my things. I was keen to get back on the narrow road and to experience again the growing inner calm that comes from long summer days spent in nature. I filled my water bottle with this water worthy of Babylon, and set off for the foothills without even having the chance to thank my sleeping host.

After an hour I stopped briefly at the ruins of an old smithy that stood by the side of a trickling stream. The stream was unbelievably pure; it bobbled and jogged over pebbles and stones, delighting the birds that landed to wash and drink in its cool waters. I opened my guidebook and read the legend that this was where Gassan, the great swordsmith, had made his swords, tempering them with a hiss in the frozen water of the stream that rose only a few feet from his house. His skill had been so great that his swords had been prized all over the world.

I sat on a rock and ate a millet cake and reflected that the mythical Gassan must have known the stream possessed some special energy, which was why he had located his smithy there.

I opened the book of Japanese poetry that I had brought from home, but the beauty of the scene quite eclipsed any poetry and I laid the book to one side. I finished my meal, marvelling at the tranquillity of the place, and then moved on into the sunshine of the dying plains.

After a long morning of sweaty toil wading through the tall grass under the heartless, indifferent gaze of the sun I finally broke through into the wild orchard groves of the foothills. There were cherry trees and orange trees, and I stopped to pick some choice fruits. Their taste was exquisite. Their juices overflowed from my mouth and ran down my sunburnt neck.

It wasn't obvious where the path went next, but perhaps because my spirits were so high from crossing the grass, instead of pausing to look at the map I recklessly pressed straight on into the wood, assuming that I would pick up the path again and that it would deliver me safely to the next temple.

Half an hour later, with the euphoria of the shining bronze fields a forgotten memory, I found myself skirting the perimeter of a huge commercial orchard. Dizzied by the insistent uphill climb and the constant waterfall of dappled sunlight that poured down on me from all sides through the forest canopy, I paused for a moment to catch my breath and wipe the sweat from my forehead. Lines upon lines of carefully pruned citrus trees were arranged in neat terraces over the curve of the hill off into the distance as far as the eye could see. Every tree appeared to be identical, clipped low to resemble an upturned sake cup, small and stout for easy picking.

The ground beneath the trees was bare, scorched of all organic matter. Not a blade of grass could be seen on the dark earth, not a mole nor a mouse, nor even a worm, could have made its home there, and not a single bird hopped on the ground or flew in the air.

The effect was to make the measureless orchard look like an endless Tokyo car park, or a production line for strange lampshades that had been magically lowered into the midst of this remote wood.

I dabbed my forehead and looked at my watch. It was mid-afternoon. By now I should have been turning north, but somewhere on the dreamy ocean of grass I had lost my way and, as I laboured up the hillside hugging the fence of the parade-ground-like orchard, my pace slowed to a crawl. Finally, after much resistance, I had to admit the truth to myself: I was completely and utterly lost.

Standing in the relative cool of the woods with the sound of my own breathing the only thing to disturb the near perfect silence, I began to take stock of my situation. I realized that I had used the last of my water from the temple well and I urgently needed to find more. Perhaps I hadn't got as far as I had planned or perhaps this was just a particularly long stretch of the march – either way there was no sign of the next temple. I would have to find alternative accommodation. I was on the brow of a gentle undulation in the landscape and I could see across the wooded valley below to what looked like a small collection of dwellings. There weren't supposed to be any hamlets or smallholdings on my route, but the sun was now way past its zenith and before too long it would be getting dark.

I decided that the most sensible thing would be to head straight for the houses and throw myself on the comfort of strangers. It had been a beautiful September day and there had been absolutely no sign of rain, but I didn't relish the idea of sleeping out in the woods, in the dark, and in any case, I had to find a source of water.

Despite my best attempt to follow a straight line down into the valley and up the other side, after two hours of walking through the trees I still hadn't managed to reach the village and I still hadn't found water. No doubt, if I had been brought up in the countryside, all sorts of tell-tale signs would have led me to a spring practically at my feet, but I might as well have been standing in the middle of a desert instead of in a luscious wood. Everywhere I turned there were trees – trees and undergrowth. I cursed myself for having lost my head in the reverie of sunshine earlier in the day.

Suddenly I thought I saw in the distance a small figure moving between the trees. Without hesitating, I headed towards the apparition. A few minutes later, I stumbled out of the wood and onto the narrow plateau of an orchard terrace.

It was an unusual orchard, like none that I had seen before on my journey through Shikoku, and at first sight I assumed that it must have fallen into disuse several years before. The trees were in a state of joyful abandon; the branches were ragged and tangled and they had long ago outgrown the order that must have once been imposed upon them by a farmer's secateurs, and succulent fruits hung half hidden within the folds of the leaves.

And it wasn't just the state of the trees that was puzzling: the orchard floor, instead of being clear earth devoid of all organic matter, as was the normal practice in the commercial orchards, was a riot of vegetation. A thick blanket of clover carpeted the ground and I could make out the leaves and flowers of many different kinds of plants all jostling for space amongst the confusion.

The last rays of sunshine were breaking through the wood behind me and the whole scene was one of breathtaking natural profusion. Perhaps because I had just spent a week seeing nothing but the neatly manicured orchards of Shikoku the wild scene had a profound effect on me. It was a vision from a fairy tale. No one farmed like this today.

Some people say that when you lose your way you do so for a reason. Your deeper mind, which is better attuned to the truth of the world than your conscious mind, has decided that your life is heading in the wrong direction and that something must finally be done.

Unconstrained by time and space your deeper mind works out a new plan that will take you back to the source of all truth, for it views your conscious mind as a wayward younger sibling who sometimes needs to be guided back on track. More often than not it neglects to explain its plan, knowing from bitter experience that the conscious mind will ignore and overrule its seemingly irrelevant advice.

But if I had not strayed from the path to the temple I would never have wandered into the wood; I would never have known the tastes of its exquisite wild fruits; I would never have stumbled upon the magical orchard; and my life would have continued on down its well-trodden path. But instead I had let myself stray from that path and now I found myself wandering alone through a wild orchard.

About twenty yards away, crouching amongst the undergrowth at the base of a citrus tree, was a man. He could not have been more than thirty years old, probably younger, but because of my relative youth he seemed old to me. I was very relieved to see another human being. As I approached him, I hailed him in my rudimentary Japanese. Alert as a rabbit, his head shot up and turned to find the source of the voice. He must have been very surprised to see a stranger appear from the bushes, doubly so as I was a foreigner. Much to my amazement he answered me in accented, but otherwise perfect English.

"Hello. Are you lost?"

He was short and wiry but he moved with enormous vitality. In a second he had slipped through the trees and come closer to inspect me better. He was wearing traditional clothes: cotton shirt and trousers, and sandals made of plant fibre; he looked as if he had stepped out of a painting from the Tokugawa period. His bright eyes regarded me with curiosity. Much relieved that we could speak in English, I tried to explain my predicament.

"Yes. I'm lost. I have no idea where I am."

The sound of my own voice surprised me. I suddenly realized that not a word had passed my lips for several days.

"I am walking the pilgrims' route. I ran out of water and I think I might have strayed from the path. The next stop was supposed to be Kashinoki. I'm sorry to walk into your farm like this."

The farmer was clearly a shy man, for now that he was standing close to me he didn't look me in the eye at all but tilted his head down and seemed to look past me. Despite this, he spoke to me with a smile on his face.

"Kashinoki is not so far from here. But it's too far to walk now."

I had grown up in Oxford, but had spent many of my childhood holidays in my uncle's cottage in rural Scotland and so was used to the ways of those who lived their lives in the outdoors. The farmer's combination of an awkward manner and decisive speech reminded me of so many of the country folk that I had met whilst roaming the Highlands.

"It will be dark in twenty minutes. Come – you can stay on my farm."

With an enormous sense of relief I accepted the farmer's generous offer and followed him down the path that wove its way through the orchard. It was good to be out of the wood and a farmhouse would make a welcome change from a temple floor.

The farmer spoke little as we walked. He looked this way and that, casting his eye over the orchard and occasionally pausing to inspect the leaves of the trees or examine the undergrowth at our feet. I walked several paces behind him, envious of his easy gait. My shoulders were sore from the rubbing of the straps of my backpack and my feet hurt. He seemed to glide through the orchard like a forest sprite.

When we arrived at the farm buildings, he explained that he slept in the mud-walled hut opposite the stone farmhouse, but that I could sleep in the main building next to the hearth. I can't remember why now, although it was clear to me straight away that this was his family farm, he must have been born under the eaves of the farmhouse, and his family must have lived there for centuries.

The farmhouse itself was in impeccable order: the dishes were washed, the floor swept and there was not a speck of dust to be seen anywhere. The sight of a cooking pot and a neat pile of eggs and freshly picked vegetables cheered my spirits, and it was only then that I realized how hungry I was. Cooking utensils were neatly stacked next to the hearth.

I removed my boots. He placed a wooden water pitcher next to me and offered me peach tea from a pot that hung over the fireplace. I noticed then that his skin glowed with good health, his buttons were solidly sewn and his clothes were looked after with such care as to make them appear to be almost brand new.

He said that he had work to finish in the orchard before dinner and that I should make myself comfortable.

I sat down, barefoot, nursing the delicious tea between my hands and enjoying the sense of peace provided by the stone walls, the small fire and the modest furniture.

It was a relief to be out of the woods and now that I had water in my belly and the prospect of dinner and even a bed for the night, my mind began to relax. Looking around me I started to wonder about the farmer and his life. Did he have a wife? It would be most unusual for someone of his age to live alone. Where were all the farm workers? And why was the orchard so wild and unkempt, so unlike all the other orchards that I'd seen on Shikoku? He clearly worked hard and was tidy, that much was certain. His home habits and self-discipline appeared to be as ascetic as those of the monks in their temples back on the path. And as for his perfect English, that was indeed a mystery.

"My name is Takeshi Fumimoto."

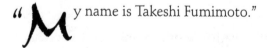

The farmer was smiling at me, looking down at me from above. I had fallen asleep in front of the fire.

"This is my family farm. I am from the village of Fumimoto, which is two miles away, down the hill and along the valley. It is an honour to have a pilgrim in my house."

I lifted myself hurriedly onto my elbow with an embarrassed smile and shook the sleep from my head. The farmer raised his right hand very gently as if to stop me and smiled. He had a kind, peaceful face.

"It is good to rest. Walking the pilgrims' route is hard in September. Too much sun. I am preparing some dinner. You must be hungry."

He deposited something at my feet.

"Here are some slippers. The biggest I could find."

Outside I could see through the windows that the sun was now low in the sky. Despite my hunger I felt refreshed and so sat up and in a gulp finished the remains of my now cold peach tea. The farmer looked at me as a doctor looks at a patient.

"More?"

"No. Thanks. It was lovely. And thank you for the slippers."

We sat in silence for some time whilst he prepared and chopped vegetables for the pot. The farmer, and indeed the entire farm, seemed to exist in a state of incredible peace.

I was very lucky, I reflected. Not many of the farmers round here would have taken me in and I was quite certain that there wouldn't have been another farmer for miles around who spoke English. Farming anywhere in the world was a tough business and rural people by nature were cautious, suspicious folk. Furthermore, even in Tokyo, let alone in the wilds of the Japanese countryside, foreigners were regarded with ambivalence at best. They were strange beings, responsible for the humiliating defeat of the Emperor in the war, and they were also the bringers of a new and deeply unsettling way of life.

I could contain my curiosity no longer.

"Forgive me for asking, Fumimoto-san, but how is it that you speak such perfect English?"

For a second the farmer's gentle gaze lifted from his work before returning quickly to focus on the pot.

Without looking up again he spoke solemnly.

"Please, call me Takeshi. What is your name?"

I had disturbed the perfect calm of the peaceful stone room with a question. Now, clearly he felt justified in encroaching on my privacy by asking me my name. I felt ashamed of myself. I had been so wrapped up in my thoughts that I hadn't introduced myself before.

"I'm so sorry. My name is James."

The farmer's eyes flickered up again. He smiled at me briefly.

"Like the Saint James. The patron saint of pilgrims."

I laughed with surprise.

"Yes. But how do you know that?"

The farmer paused in his work again and, with a knowing smile, for the first time his gaze stayed on me.

"Now I have two questions to answer. I will answer them both together: I was taught English by a priest, a missionary who lived in the village."

He continued to stir the pot and added as an afterthought: "I was also trained as a scientist several years ago."

We fell into silence once more.

"May I have some more tea?"

The farmer put down the knife he was using and began to move towards the hearth. Quickly, I jumped up and unhooked the kettle from its hanger above the fire.

"I can get it. Would you like some?"

He smiled at me warmly.

"No thank you. I have some here."

I poured out the tea, replaced the kettle on its hanger and sat down again in silence. The company of this man brought me a feeling of immense peace.

Over dinner I volunteered a few observations on the countryside through which I had passed that day and I told him a little about my life. I was hoping that if I talked he might venture his own opinions, but for whatever reason he chose not to. He listened with interest and nodded politely but didn't tell me anything more about himself.

After dinner he tidied up, refusing all offers of help. His only question was to ask, with a very grave expression on his face, if I had enjoyed the meal.

"It was delicious," I said with genuine enthusiasm, picking the last grains of rice from the inside of my rice bowl. This answer pleased him greatly.

"It was all grown here: the rice from the fields below, the vegetables and the seven herbs of spring from the orchard above. The only things that were not grown here were the soya beans for the soy sauce. Right now it is not practical to make it on the farm. There are not enough people."

For a second I thought that I caught a sad look on his face, but he turned back to his work, replacing the cleaned and wiped pans in their proper places by the hearth. Something about this curious man intrigued me and I wanted to learn more. He seemed to exude self-assurance; I can't explain quite why I thought so but, in a way that is absent in most people, I felt that he seemed to know exactly why he was here on earth.

My enthusiasm for the food was real.

"The hard-boiled egg was exquisite. It reminded me of the eggs that I had in my childhood. For some reason they don't taste like that any more. Neither here nor back home."

He stopped what he was doing and graced me with his steady profound gaze.

"The eggs come from my hens. They are an old Japanese breed called Black Crow. I think I am the last person in Ehime Prefecture to keep them, maybe the last person on Shikoku. If that is the case then I am also the last person in Japan. They are small and skinny. They wander through the orchard and provide me with free manure ... and they have a special trick. They peck the insects off the leaves without damaging the plants at all. They turn the pests into food for the vegetables."

Suddenly he caught himself and fell silent, but there was something about his clear way of speaking that had given me a glimpse out over the landscape of his life. It was as if clouds had parted momentarily, uncovering a wonderful mountain-top view before closing again in darkness. I wanted him to speak. I was intrigued to hear his thoughts. I knew that if I stayed on the subject of farming he would talk.

"But why does no one else keep the Black Crow any more?"

He paused again as if he was choosing his words very carefully, suspecting correctly that I knew nothing of farming or nature.

"The new chickens lay many more eggs. But they get fed with feed pellets and are kept in coops day and night. It is not just the big farms that do that. Even on the family farms they would rather toss out a handful of pellets than risk them wandering around and getting eaten or lost."

I felt, quite distinctly, that although this man was talking about hens, he was in fact telling me about something else, something of far greater significance, which had enormous implications for myself and indeed for the whole world.

"But after two summers they stop laying, whilst the Black Crow continue for years. When the time comes, the farmers cook the hens in a pot. Why do they stop laying? The farmers do not know or care.

The hens are cut off from nature on all sides. Who can finally tell?"

He took my plate and cup.

"I'm glad you liked your dinner. I have a little work to do. Please have some more tea or sleep. I will try to be as quiet as possible."

Leaving me by the hearth, he tidied up the last things and then sat down at a small wooden work table in the corner of the room.

The rest of the evening was spent in almost complete silence. At the table, the farmer took out a box that contained many small bags. Each bag held a different type of seed. One by one, he emptied each bag onto a different dish before carefully arranging the dishes in a row on the far side of the workbench. I poured myself some more tea and took out my diary, but I wasn't really in the mood for writing.

With all the seed dishes arranged, he left the room through the door into the garden and came back a moment later carrying a large earthenware jar. Removing the lid from the jar, he fished his hand inside and took out a glistening lump of clay, which I suspected he had dug up from the hillside. He pinched off a piece of clay in his fingertips and then proceeded to take a seed from each dish and embed it within the moist clay before rolling the whole concoction very gently between the palms of his hands.

Tentatively, I asked him what he was doing and he muttered one word only: "Seedball". He was deep in concentration. I wanted to offer my help, but I thought that if I asked he might feel bound to let me try and then I would slow down his whole operation whilst he tried to teach me what to do. He worked with speed and delicacy and I didn't see him drop a single seed, even though many of them were extremely small, and he worked at his task for more than an hour.

Finally, having filled a large bamboo basket with seedballs, he returned the remaining seeds to their bags, put the bags back in the sturdy box and carried the earthenware pot back into the garden. By the time that he had finished his work I was already almost asleep, but out of the corner of my eye I saw him steal back into the farmhouse and carefully extinguish his work lamp. The room fell into almost complete darkness. The last remaining embers of the fire cast a weak, flickering light. Only now did his day seem to be finally coming to an end.

Basho says that every haiku should convey *sabi*, which can be loosely translated into English as "loneliness". He didn't mean the loneliness of the shipwrecked sailor, or the loneliness of the night watchman who must stand guard at his dangerous post all night long in the cold; he was referring to a loneliness of a different order, a loneliness that is far more tragic and devastating.

If a soldier walks off to battle in a brand new suit of armour, but that soldier is an old soldier with thin legs and white hair, then that is *sabi*. Or if a young man picks a beautiful rose and gives it to a woman with whom he is in love, but she despises him and discards the rose in a ditch, then the rose lying in the ditch also has *sabi*. Or if a well-intentioned man lives in an outsize dream but doesn't realize it, then that too might be *sabi*. But as hard as I thought about the farmer, and despite what I expected to find, I could detect no trace of *sabi* anywhere.

I rolled over and turned my back to the dying embers and thought of the brilliant sunshine of the plains that had almost reduced me to delirium, and of the wild fruit trees of the woods whose juices still stained my shirt. I thought of the old monk in the derelict temple, who would now be curled up alone on the cold stone floor, and I thought of the well that stood in the temple yard; and its cool dark waters that could quench any thirst and, before images faded altogether from my weary mind, I thought of the seedballs nestled in their bamboo basket and the fabulous forests of vegetables that they promised to bring. But most of all I thought of the farmer.

The following day I was woken once again by the sound of the farmer's busy activity. He was squatting over the hearth, arranging pots and pouring fresh water into the kettle. He must have sensed that I had stirred, for he turned his head to look at me.

"Good morning. Did you sleep well?"

He had flung open the large door to the garden and light was streaming into the room, along with a very gentle breeze that was laden with scents from the fields. I could hear birdsong. I smiled dreamily and then gingerly moved my limbs under the blanket. I was relieved to find that my aches and pains had completely vanished and I was feeling very much less weary.

"Yes. I slept extremely well."

He continued to potter around, coming in and out of the door to the garden and then standing in the doorway and surveying the view of the garden and fields beyond. I sensed a change in his mood from the day before. I couldn't put my finger on it exactly, but I felt he seemed more open, more relaxed. As if to confirm my feelings he spoke again with a smile on his face.

"We have had a very good omen this morning."

I sat up and rubbed my eyes and discovered next to me a cup of hot tea and a bowl of gruel with fresh herbs and vegetables. Hungrily I tucked into the breakfast, wondering what he might be referring to. When I had finished my food he interrupted his activity and came over to me to pick up the empty bowl and cup.

I bowed my head and handed them to him. "Thank you. That was absolutely delicious."

A radiant smile lit up his face.

"When you are ready I will show you. This is something very special."

A look of puzzlement must have crossed my face, for he nodded as if to reinforce his point.

"Really. It is very special indeed. It can be no accident that you arrived last night."

Intrigued, I folded the blanket and put it next to my pillow. While I was doing this the farmer swept out the fireplace and rekindled a fresh summer fire. Then, seeing that I was ready, he ushered me with him over to the door to the garden.

I stepped into the warm sunlight and looked out over the garden and fields, and what I saw left me speechless. Covering every inch of the vegetable garden and the rice fields below – a space probably totalling two acres or more – was a miraculous blanket of silk, shimmering and glistening in the morning sun. I had never seen anything like it before. Without taking his eyes off the sparkling vision, the farmer spoke.

"Spider webs."

I gasped in amazement. He nodded his explanation.

"They appear overnight, only very rarely, once every seven years. And by the end of the day they will all be gone."

I shook my head in wonder.

"They're so beautiful."

He turned to me with a smile. "You see it can be no accident that you came."

I was still staring in amazement at the beauty of it all.

"But why does this happen?" I said, gesturing towards the fields.

"Go and look. Every square foot of ground contains hundreds of thousands of tiny spiders. Altogether there must be millions of them, but they will all vanish and tomorrow not a single one will be left."

He stepped over to the edge of the vegetable garden and squatted down to examine the extraordinary silk blanket.

"You see these fine strands of web? They break off and wave about in the air. Then the spiders clamber up from underneath and cling to the strands with all their strength – six, seven, sometimes ten of them on one strand, like this one here. Over the course of the day the threads come loose from their moorings and carry the spiders aloft, floating away to who knows where."

"But that's incredible."

Then I noticed something strange. A quarter of a mile away, there was a fence that marked the boundary of the farmer's rice field, and beyond the fence lay a commercial farm. For some reason, there wasn't a single strand of silk beyond the fence, not one single spider planning its daring escape.

"Why hasn't it happened in the other fields?"

A shadow passed over the farmer's face. For the first time since I had met him he looked unhappy.

"People think that they know nature, but they don't. That is why."

We fell into silence. I wanted to ask him to explain his cryptic comment, but I didn't feel it was the right time. After a minute or so he spoke again.

"When I was a very young boy, I remember someone came running to the house in the morning asking us why we had covered our fields in a silk net. We didn't know what he was talking about until we stepped outside. That was the last time I saw this sight. Then my father too started to use pesticides; after that, we never saw the spiders again. Until today."

I was glad to see him smile once more. His natural good nature had returned.

"No one understands these things. One year it is spiders, the next it is frogs and the year after that it is toads. Nature is too deep to fathom, its patterns are too intricate. But nowadays the farmer focuses on one tiny thing, like controlling seed-blight. He sprays a chemical and by accident he wipes out ten million spiders. And because of this the insects that spiders would otherwise have eaten come and destroy our precious crops. So, the only thing left to do is to kill everything."

He looked at me and smiled sadly. "It's a curious way to farm."

We stood in silence marvelling at the wondrous scene until the farmer turned back to me once more.

"But now I must work."

Urgently I spoke. "Perhaps I can help? I would be glad to help and I could do with a rest from the walking."

In truth I could have pressed on. I wasn't so tired that I had to rest, but I desperately wanted to stay. It was so peaceful here and I was intrigued by the life of the farmer. Everything that he did or said seemed to spring from one central source of belief, as if at some point in the past he had experienced a true insight into the workings of the world and it was by the light of this insight that he lived his every moment. I wanted to learn more, I wanted to find out what he thought.

He smiled at me as if it was the most natural request in the world and replied that I was welcome to stay if I wanted.

"But first we must get you some proper shoes or you will crush all the young shoots and stamp the earth to dust."

I thought that he was pleased that I had asked to stay, though I couldn't tell for sure. It was equally possible that he simply didn't mind either way. He certainly seemed more relaxed. I thought that perhaps the fact that my arrival had coincided with the return of the spiders made him look more favourably on me – I didn't know.

I followed him over to a cupboard that stood by the back door and watched him rummage around, looking for a pair of shoes. With his back still turned to me he continued to talk.

"In America and Europe, and even in Japan these days, people drive huge pieces of machinery over the land every day. Some of those combine harvesters and tractors weigh ten tons or more; it is little wonder that the soil turns to finely pressed dust ..."

Shoes of many different sizes were stacked in neat piles in the cupboard. I looked down at my heavy walking boots.

"What we really need are great clods of rich soil, like chunks of horse manure. Each clod is a little world of its own, filled with life, and further down, moles and worms will make their homes. Then the soil will be rich in nutrition and from our tiny seeds things as dense and hard as potatoes and turnips will be summoned into life; strong crops will grow that will be able to withstand disease, and the pests will be kept at bay by the wildlife that will make our fields their home."

He turned round and handed me a pair of soft fibre shoes. I sat down on the ground and wrenched off my heavy boots and slipped into the farmer's shoes. I couldn't prevent myself from smiling when I stood up; I felt as if I was in bare feet.

"They're so light!"

The farmer smiled in return.

It was one of those truly uplifting mornings that can only be experienced in the depths of the countryside. The air was crisp and fresh, the light was superabundant and the birds were singing joyfully in the trees. Below us the fields dressed in their fabulous silver robes shimmered in the sunlight.

On a low work-table next to the back wall of the house was a large bamboo tray. The tray was covered in seedballs. The farmer explained that they had been left out in the open air for two days so that the clay would dry a little in the sun. This way the hardened clay skin would offer the precious contents some protection from pests, but when it rained the clay would dissolve away again and the seeds would be released onto the wet soil.

He then carefully emptied the seedballs into a large basket and handed me the basket with a smile. He turned and picked out two old-fashioned scythes, which were leaning in a stack against the wall of the house, and hooked the long blades over his shoulder before we set off up the hill towards the orchard.

The Zen poets of old lived high up in the cold mountains or lost in the valleys down below. White masses of cloud piled up around the peaks, and the valleys were filled with smoky rain. The tiny houses of the woodcutters were their only neighbours and the distant sound of an axe echoing through the mountains was all that might remind them of what they had left behind.

The paths of these poets led through long gorges choked with scree and boulders. Wild rivers tumbled alongside them and mist-laden vegetation covered the canyon sides. Moss clung to the rocks on the path, which were always slippery even when there was no rain. The pines were always murmuring, the water was always trickling.

The paths led between the vines and rocky caves to huts hidden deep in the mountains where the white clouds touched the snow. When travellers looked for these paths to the clouds they could never find them, they seemed to go from sky to sky.

As I followed the farmer through the sunny fields of the orchard I was reminded of the poets of old, and I wondered if it would happen that, when I left the farm, I would never be able to find it again. I was overwhelmed by a deep sense of sadness and an urgency to experience as much as I could of its wonderful atmosphere.

Dragonflies and butterflies fluttered between us as we walked. Bumblebees, flying like old-fashioned biplanes, zigzagged this way and that, as they travelled from blossom to blossom. Beneath our feet the ground was soft; we were walking on a carpet of wild flowers and clover. Spiders, frogs, lizards and insects that I could not even begin to name bustled around in the cool shade, or ran in spirals of panic on hearing our gentle approach.

After a few minutes we passed through the orchard and stepped onto the open slopes of the hill. Weeds and grasses covered the hillside for half a mile. Higher up, the woods began again, and further down the sharp edge of a commercial rice farm ran in a straight line following the contour of the bottom of the hill. The farmer unhooked the scythes from his shoulder and turned them the right way up, and then explained to me what he was going to do.

"First we will cut down the weeds and grasses, and then we will sow the seedballs onto the bare hillside. When this is done we will return the dead weeds to the field. We will lay them on top of the seedballs as a mulch."

I wasn't sure that I understood him correctly. It was true that I knew little about farming, but I knew enough to know that if he was going to plant this hillside he would first have to kill or uproot all the weeds. Simply cutting the weeds down at ground level would not destroy them. And just tossing the seeds out to lie on top of the ground was hopeless; they would be eaten by birds and strangled by the weeds as soon as the weeds began to regrow.

I asked him if he intended to use pesticides. He said no. Would he plough the land or use fertilizer? He said he planned to do neither of those things. He had his own way.

I didn't understand. All the people of the world ploughed the land and prepared the soil and nowadays, even in Japan, farmers had begun to use pesticides and fertilizer. I had seen the evidence with my own eyes during the course of my walk. He seemed to be expecting nature to do the farming for him.

I asked him if the land belonged to him. He answered no. Did he know whose land it was? He did not know. He supposed that it belonged to the village, or perhaps it belonged to someone who didn't care about it. He himself did not care to know who the owners were and he did not mind at all if, after all his work, they came to ask for it back.

He explained that in the months to come he would cut the weeds again and the young plants that would just be sprouting from the seedballs would have a small head start on the weeds. By next year these six acres would be covered in lush green clover and the vegetables would already have started to grow.

I was unsure what to say. Questions grew in my mind – questions that I didn't feel that I could ask. Did he also use his technique in the orchard? Did that explain why the orchard looked so overgrown and abandoned? Why did he have no farm workers? And what about his rice? How did he grow that? I hadn't seen his rice paddies yet but he must certainly plough and use chemicals there.

The farmer smiled at me patiently. I had the distinct impression that he knew exactly what I was thinking. This made me feel quite uncomfortable, for I didn't want him to suspect that I doubted him and I certainly didn't want to offend him. But he didn't look offended at all.

He said that he would be glad to explain, but there was work to do. We could talk about it over lunch. In the meantime, he suggested that I take a walk in the woods. Farm work was hard and it took months to learn to use a scythe. I insisted that I would give it a go. I intended to earn my keep and besides, I was now completely fascinated.

Using his right foot like a hoof, he cleared away the weeds from the ground around his feet, revealing hard red-coloured earth.

"This soil is virtually clay right now. That is why

the wood that grows well higher up the hillside doesn't extend this far down. The soil must be improved or citrus trees will never be able to take hold. The clover, combined with the work that the plant roots will do, will act as a natural fertilizer. It will bring nutrition back to the soil and with it will come life. Worms and insects, birds and bees will follow. In five years' time the soil will be black and moist and packed with microorganisms, and in ten years this too will all be orchard, filled with chestnuts and citrus and persimmons. When nature is healthy and in balance there is no need to fear pests or disease and there is no need to plough the soil. The mosquitoes do not gather by clear streams, they gather by the stagnant waters; and lice and maggots do not infect the healthy flesh, they infect the dead and dying. Rice and barley will grow wherever there is a little good earth. They do not need the farmer with his schemes. They grew before mankind was born and they will grow long after he has gone."

He began to swing the scythe rhythmically through the air, mowing the weeds and grasses to the ground. I looked at the hard orange earth and then lifted my gaze to survey the ragged, weed-covered hillside. Shaking my head in wonder and disbelief I gripped the scythe, and banishing all other thoughts from my mind I followed his example and set to work.

After two hours I had developed large blisters on my hands, and my shoulders were aching from the unusual, repetitive motion. The sun was now high in the sky. I surveyed my handiwork. I had managed a quarter of an acre but I had not done the job well; tufts of weeds stuck up all over the place.

By now the farmer was a small figure in the distance. When he noticed that I had stopped, he trotted over the field and congratulated me on my efforts.

"That's very good. Now you deserve a rest. Come, let's go down to the farmhouse and have some tea inside, in the shade."

Sitting by the hearth next to the smouldering summer fire, I sensed that working together in the fields had created a new intimacy between us. The time was now right to ask him about his life, and with a gentle insistence I began to question him. He was not used to talking about himself – that was clear – but he had a natural and fluent way of expressing himself and as soon as he did start to speak I was instantly fascinated.

"I was born here in the farmhouse on the night of the autumn full moon in the second year of the last Emperor's reign. My father, Matsuo Fumimoto, farmed this land before me, as did his father before him. My family has lived in Ehime Prefecture for as long as anyone knows."

I poured some cool water from the pitcher and gulped it down. The farmer pressed his hands around his warm mug of tea and furrowed his brow. Gently, I encouraged him to tell his story.

"You said that you were once a scientist? How come then you have ended up as a farmer?"

He sipped his tea. I was worried that any minute he would want to get back to the fields, but he seemed relaxed and in no hurry. I sensed that he knew exactly what had to be done and how long it would take him, and that without even thinking about it he would know when he had to return to the fields. In any case, farming wasn't *work* in the sense that I understood the word. Walking the fields and tending to the land was just the way he lived; it was like sleeping or breathing. Once again a kind smile appeared on the farmer's face, but it was followed by a gentle frown.

"You ask difficult questions. If you really want me to answer them properly I have to begin at the beginning."

I looked at the blisters on my hands and then smiled back at him.

"Well, I think I may have done my last scything for the day. I would love to hear, if you can spare the time."

For reasons that I couldn't fathom, I had an instinct that the farmer's life might throw some light on my own struggle. He paused to collect his thoughts and then, very slowly, he began to speak in his gentle voice.

"When I was a child on this farm, all I knew was nature. I didn't know it as one knows things that one learns at school. I didn't ever have to learn about it. I had no particular interest in memorizing the workings of the seasons or what foods are available when. I just knew it all and I knew it better than I do today."

For a moment he paused as if working out how best to explain his life to me, and then he began again.

"But everything changed when I was eighteen. I left the farm for the first time to travel to the city of Yokohama to take up a place at the Yokohama Agricultural Institute. I had been a good student at the village school and the teachers had told my parents that I should go to the city. It would be wrong to keep me in the stifling existence of a traditional farm."

The farmer chuckled at his own words and then continued.

"My father was particularly enthusiastic about me going. He had just begun to embrace the new chemical farming that had arrived from abroad. He saw it as the salvation for small farms like our own and he thought that I would become an expert in the use of pesticides and fertilizers. But I didn't want to go at all. In fact I was so nervous about going that I thought of running away to live in the forest, but my mother and father gave me no choice. The Yokohama Agricultural Institute was extremely prestigious and as far as they were concerned it was a great opportunity. Even now I can remember the constant stream of visitors coming to the farm to congratulate my parents on their good fortune.

"For days I hid in the fields or wandered in the woods. I didn't want to leave the farm. I didn't want to go to Yokohama. But my parents were never going to listen to me. The start of term was coming and soon I would have to go."

Gently, I interrupted him.

"But why didn't you want to go?"

"I had no wish to study farming in the big city. I didn't want to get locked in a classroom day and night. All I knew was nature and the outdoor life."

I still couldn't believe that a farmer's son wouldn't have been over the moon about going to the big city. I thought that that was what all country people dreamed of. Having grown up in a small town myself, I had always yearned to journey to the big city. And I was young and so naturally I assumed that other people's ambitions would be similar to my own.

"But you must have liked Yokohama when you got there? It must have been exciting for you?"

The farmer smiled at me patiently.

"My first experience of Yokohama was through the train window. I remember for a long time all I could see was little houses. Then after an hour or so the houses were replaced by taller and taller buildings, until finally they became so tall I could no longer see the sky, and by the time the train approached the centre of the city it was sliding in and out of tunnels, under elevated roads, and squeezing its way between enormous tower blocks of steel and concrete. I had never seen anything like it before."

The farmer paused for a moment. He seemed to be lost in thought, remembering his first experience of the big city.

"When I finally found my way to the Agricultural Institute I was given a small room in one of the tower blocks next to Yamate Park, on the bluff that overlooks the harbour. Have you ever been to Yokohama?"

I shook my head.

"Well, it is a great city with a huge harbour, filled with ships that are constantly bustling about, so the view from my room was magnificent. The room was actually a very peaceful place – perfect for study and thought. But that didn't mean I felt at home there. Every day I went to the laboratory next to the apartment block to attend classes or to study the infectious diseases of rice through a microscope. As you can imagine, it was quite difficult for me to go from the farm to a lonely life in a tower block in Yokohama, but that is the way of the modern world."

"What did they teach you?"

The farmer sighed.

"They tried to teach us the modern scientific view of life."

I must have looked puzzled. The farmer tried to explain himself.

"What I mean is that they tried to teach us that it is possible to know nature and that it is possible to break nature down into parts and understand how nature works – just as we can understand how a pocket watch works by taking it to pieces."

I listened in fascination as the farmer continued his tale.

"Even today I still clearly remember the first morning of classes. Professor Mitsubishi, one of the most famous professors in the whole of Japan, came to give an introductory talk about agriculture. Even then Professor Mitsubishi was already a very old man. He looked as if he hadn't left Yokohama for many years, let alone actually set foot on a farm. The curtains were drawn and the lights were turned off and the Professor's assistant turned on a slide projector. I had never seen anything like this before. Projected onto the white screen were ten or twelve amoebas. They pulsated with life and they were constantly moving around. They reminded me of jellyfish from the Inland Sea, bobbing on the tide.

"We watched these little creatures and the Professor talked a great deal about food and energy and the importance of using pesticides and chemical fertilizer, and then he prodded one of the amoebas with the tip of a sharp needle. The amoeba's skin became very hard and its movement became much weaker. I couldn't understand what was going on.

"The Professor – in fact all of the staff at the Institute – liked to use the new words and phrases that had been brought from America and Europe. I remember he kept using the words 'evolution' and 'competition' and the phrase 'survival of the fittest', whilst at the same time jabbing at the amoeba again and again. Its rigidity increased still further. Around the amoeba swam its brothers and sisters, beating like hearts. But now the amoeba hardly moved at all. It was like a bee that had survived into the winter; it just lay there and let itself get pushed around until finally it shrank into itself, like a little old village woman who had led an unhappy life. Then it stopped moving at all."

The farmer sighed and shook his head at the memory.

"I left the lecture feeling quite sick. What has this got to do with farming? I thought. What's more, I was angry. It was the season for mushroom hunting. At the farm they would be missing me, I knew where all the best places were. I should have been there, helping."

The farmer paused again and poured himself some water, which he proceeded to sip slowly as he reflected on his past. I was appalled by the story of the amoebas. No wonder the farmer didn't like Yokohama and the Institute.

"Did it all get better? Maybe you were just homesick?" I said.

The farmer put the cup down and, looking me in the eye, he began again.

"I had no choice but to make the best I could of it. I could not return home. The shame would have been too great. Every day, I sat at my desk at the laboratory window with Yokohama city stretching away beneath me. I worked all the time. On more than one occasion I worked so hard that I actually passed out at my desk. I wasn't used to spending so much time alone. At the farm there was always someone around.

"After a month of this lonely existence I finally left the laboratory late one evening and went out into the city night. I have to admit it was exciting. It was the first time I had explored the city and I walked for hours and hours through the neon lanes until finally I followed a crowd into a bar. It was dark and smoky inside and the music was almost deafening. Although I had very little money from my parents, I bought a drink, and sat on my own at a table. I still hadn't got into the habit of taking off my coat as soon as I was indoors so I received quite a few funny looks.

"Next to me was a group of four young salary-men. They were about my age, maybe a little older. They were dressed in black suits and they were sitting in big leather armchairs. On the table in front of them were lots of empty beer bottles. I watched them as they drank bottle after bottle and laughed and shouted at each other. They put their feet on the edge of the table and leant back on their chairs. They bought cigars from the waiter. They tried to light them and almost set fire to each other's hair. That made them laugh even harder. They puffed on the cigars, coughing and pointing at each other. They fell backwards off their chairs. Their black suits were soaked with beer.

"Accidentally I caught the eye of the loudest of the group. I smiled at him. They all began to look at me and talk about me and then they started to point at me and shout. I continued to smile at them and stood up. One of them leant over to touch me, but instead he fell flat on his face, hitting the floor with a crash of bottles. I turned around and left.

"Outside, the sky was the colour of a peacock's neck. I felt tired and lost. Where was the harbour? Where was the bluff? When I finally returned home, I decided not to go out to bars any more. I resolved to devote myself to study instead.

"The days went by and the routine was more or less the same. We studied aspects of nature and aspects of plants and soil. We broke them down into constituent parts: leaves, roots, seeds and so on. We broke down the list of predators and the list of things that the plants would need: the vitamins, the micronutrients, the sunlight, the carbon dioxide. The teachers seemed to think that dividing nature into parts was the natural thing to do, but I thought that it was wrong."

I was confused by the farmer's words. Yet he smiled and sighed.

"The goal of our study was to be able to create the perfect rice field, without any pests but still containing the correct amount of nutrients and vitamins. The problem is that you can no more create a perfect rice field by taking the rice plants out of nature than you can create the perfect human by taking a baby from its home and placing it in a heated white room and feeding it synthetic food. Rice plants and humans need their natural environments. They need coughs and colds and seed-blight to toughen them up; they need foods rich in nutrition and soil rich in diverse nutrients; they don't need a vitamin pill and plain white bread or three tons of nitrogen phosphate every spring.

"Studying nature under a microscope and then copying the parts of it that we think are good will never work. The human mind will never be able to understand nature fully – what appears from the outside to be a pest in fact turns out to be a critical part of nature's process. But nevertheless, day in, day out in the laboratory, that is exactly what we tried to do.

"I was reasonably good at it but I didn't like it. It didn't make sense to me. At the time I didn't really know why I didn't like it, I just felt instinctively that it was all wrong and wished that I was back on the farm where I didn't have to think about anything; where the days went by and I was always busy. But I could never escape the thought that I didn't fit in.

"I remember one conversation I had particularly well. It marked a turning point in my life in Yokohama. I was standing in the queue at the Agricultural Institute canteen looking at the food that was on display, trying to decide what to choose for lunch. It was always the same processed stuff and the selection was very limited. It was most unappetizing for a country boy like myself.

"Nowadays, I know that there are two ways in which a person can starve. I have had time to think about the world and I understand it better. People can starve from lack of calories, for example when the harvest fails, or when there is a war and the food supply is interrupted; or they can starve inwardly, from lack of nutrition. The human body needs many micronutrients that do not appear in city food. The body has to have these tiny amounts of metals and minerals, just as much as it has to have water and energy. It simply cannot function properly without these things and its chemistry becomes unbalanced.

"When people have a shortage of these things, they become desperate, even violent. They don't realize what the cause of their problems is because outwardly they look OK. They are not thin and emaciated, but it is the same thing. All around the modern world, people are inwardly starving and it is having a devastating effect on their happiness and peace of mind. It's no exaggeration to say that inward starvation is causing wars and crime, as hungry people lash out in desperation. At the time I didn't understand all this, I just instinctively knew that it was not good to eat the same five things every day.

"On that particular afternoon the chef, who was dressed in smart white clothes like a hospital surgeon, was standing on the far side of the brightly lit stainless-steel serving counter. His arms were crossed over his chest, his face was wearing a stern expression.

"You have to remember, I was only eighteen and I didn't really understand how the world worked, so I tried to explain to the chef that there were many other, better kinds of food than those that he was offering. I wasn't trying to criticize him. I was just being enthusiastic. I was trying to help.

"'Not many people know it but even lice and fleas are very good food,' I began. 'There are many recipes that I know from home that use lice and fleas. In fact, almost all the insects of the Japanese Archipelago are very nutritious and they often have special medicinal properties, too. Did you know that ground-up lice from the shores of the Inland Sea are a cure for epilepsy and that ladybirds will almost always calm the nerves? At home, if someone is feeling anxious or out of sorts, we give them a little ladybird tea and straight away their feelings of anxiety will pass. Food and medicine are opposite sides of the same coin.'

"I beamed happily at the chef. I was so glad to finally find someone that I could talk to. 'And insect larvae are edible too,' I continued. 'And they are really filled with goodness. But they have to be alive. The tastiest of all the tiny creatures are silkworms. They are as exquisite as the kimono of a princess. People only think they are revolting. It is the same with the chickens and ducks that are reared in batteries in the dark, like the ones that you serve here. They are force fed and injected with chemicals. People think that they taste good, but they don't. Their cousins the wild birds – the pheasants and guinea fowl and pigeons – taste much better and they are more nutritious. They have a diverse diet of wild food. The imprisoned birds eat pellets of synthetic matter. It is very sad. And it is the same with vegetables. The vegetables closer to their wild ancestors are richer in flavour and in nutrition. In the lily family, garlic and leek are better than anything, but people prefer the green onion and bulb onion. People are confused. They prefer the flavours of foods that are raised using chemicals, they prefer the tastes of sugar and salt.'

"I remember, a crowd had gathered by this point. I carried on chattering away. They were staring at me and giggling. The chef watched me in silence. I felt very uncomfortable. Had I spoken for too long? Perhaps I had offended him. I waited to hear what he had to say, but he did not even blink. I bowed quickly and, picking up my tray with its bowl of white rice and vegetables, I turned to face the canteen.

"At that moment one of my classmates hailed me. What a relief to see a friendly face. The classmate had just finished lunch. He was carrying his tray back to the counter. He had something to say to me.

"'Are you coming to the lecture after lunch? It's by the Minister of Agriculture. It's about your home prefecture. It's about Ehime. They have great plans for it. They want to develop it into the most advanced prefecture in Japan.'"

"I was very eager to hear what the Minister of Agriculture had to say about Ehime. I wolfed down my lunch and hurried along to the lecture. The Minister had a loud, important-sounding voice.

"'Ladies and Gentlemen', he said, 'let me begin by clearly stating our goals. We will create, in Ehime Prefecture, the perfect modern environment for growing rice. To develop to its potential, rice needs energy. Energy is communication. The sun communicates with the leaves and creates chlorophyll. Chlorophyll is the information that carries life and energy around the plant's telephone exchange of capillaries ...'

"I stared around the room in bafflement. What strange words the Minister used! He didn't seem to be talking about farming at all. In fact he didn't seem to be talking about anything.

"'To begin with we must complete our study of rice growing in the Prefecture,' he continued. 'We must record every detail about current practices on each and every farm. We must know the exact temperature of the leaves of each plant. We must know at what angle the sunlight strikes the plant, how much sunlight it receives a day, how long it has spent in the flooded paddy before being transferred to the growing field. All this we must know. In addition, we must fully understand the soil conditions: what the salinity is, what the alkalinity is, what nutrients are in abundance and, of course, what nutrients are lacking. With all this information, we will then be able to decide on a dietary programme for our rice. We will then go on to study the predators and the weeds. What kinds of predators are there? What do the predators themselves eat, how much damage do they cause a year? What weeds are there, which predators destroy the weeds, and so on. Finally, we will synthesize this data and create a development plan. The development plan can best be thought of as a healthcare scheme for the crops. We will know their every need and so we will be able to administer the proper specialist care in the form of pesticides, fertilizers and intervention of other sorts. Without all this intervention, our food supplies will forever be vulnerable to the whims of nature and our yields will fall far below those achieved on foreign farms.'

"By this point I had drifted off. As hard as I tried, I could not follow what the Minister was saying. He didn't really seem to be speaking in words at all – he spoke in phrases. At home in the village, everyone had their own individual way of talking and everyone used different words and put them together in different ways, but here the Minister sounded just like all the other lecturers. All his words came together in prearranged phrases. These phrases were big and simple, but they were too big to describe my farm and too simple to describe nature. No matter what the Minister measured or how far he looked into his microscope, he would never understand. He was trying to measure the bottomless ocean with a six-foot pole!

"Besides, I had other things to think about! At the farm, the spinach would be ready by now and for dinner they would be eating the new rice and probably mackerel. And it was of course the time for crabs and squid and gingko nuts... and the time to sow the seeds for the New Year ... But the Minister was still talking.

"'When we have finally finished, Ehime will be the model prefecture. In one step it will become a utopia for rice farmers. All the needs of the rice plant will be met. All alien material, weeds, insects, animals and so on, will be exterminated. The rice will stand alone in earth purified of all extraneous matter. All that will remain is the rice plant, the soil, the sun and the nourishment that we will provide using the most up-to-date scientific methods. The most modern mechanized equipment will be employed to achieve this goal. We will link Shikoku to the rest of Japan by a brand new sea bridge, made of the newest alloys and strengthened plastoid fibres, and by a revitalized road network that will criss-cross the province like a net, dragging it out of its torpor and backwardness. Ehime Prefecture will become the most modern, and therefore the most developed, prefecture in the whole of Japan. Small-scale, self-sufficient farming will finally be wiped out. It is primitive, inefficient and backward. It must be eliminated as quickly as possible. Too many people still farm in Japan. With large modern machines and bigger farms, we will need fewer people to produce a higher yield. I promise to deliver to Ehime a modern farming environment where only ten per cent of the population work on farms, as in America and Europe.'

"At this point I was jolted from my daydream. I couldn't believe my ears. The Minister seemed to think that small farms were a bad idea and that farm workers should be doing something else. In my opinion, *all* of the people should be farmers. If everyone farmed a quarter-acre each, then the whole country would have plenty to eat and everyone would be happy.

"The Minister asked, 'Are there any questions?'

"I had many questions, but I didn't know where to begin. I wanted to explain to the Minister that he was quite wrong. I wanted to tell him about our farm and how perfect it was. But then I thought of the chef. In Japan, we have a saying – *deru kugi wa utareru* – the nail that sticks out must be hammered in. I thought of my fellow students in the queue who had laughed at me behind their hands and I thought of the chef's stern face and I decided to stay silent. The audience rose to its feet. Applause filled the hall. From that day on I hardly spoke to anyone.

"Soon after the lecture from the Minister, I stopped going to the lectures. I continued to study and I passed all of the exams, doing quite well in them. But I kept my thoughts to myself and slowly but surely over the course of the next two years I became disillusioned with the world.

"I found that I was unable to sleep and my evenings became a series of aimless wanderings. This went on for months until finally, one evening, I was sitting on a train, coming back into the city at the end of a long, tiring walk when I looked out of the window and saw amongst the concrete of Yokohama a tiny patch of green.

"It lay between the big raised intercity highway and the little local road that joined the highway to the city's main road network. It was nothing really. No more than a mere triangular wedge of land, too badly placed and strangely shaped to be put to any constructive use. Nevertheless, it was hard to believe that it was not concreted over. There was scarcely an inch of ground in the whole of Yokohama that wasn't concreted over, so it was almost miraculous that this little sliver of earth existed at all. Once upon a time it must have been farmland, but that would have been many years ago.

"I was very tired, but I sat up in my seat and looked more closely. I saw that in between the weeds and chaos of the overgrown plot healthy, tall, strong rice plants were flourishing unaided by any pesticides or fertilizer.

"I cupped my hands over the glass. Seeing the small unkempt patch of nature in the middle of the vast city was like suddenly spotting an old friend from home. I wanted to cry out with surprise. With a huge grin on my face I turned to my neighbour, but my neighbour was immersed in a comic book. I pressed my face back against the glass, with both hands curled around my eyes like binoculars. In this world beyond the window, young rice shoots were growing tall and strong: free of even the basic necessities of civilized farming, free of pesticides or fertilizer, free even of the plough – here amongst the skyscrapers and lead fumes of Yokohama!

"I was ecstatic. When the train pulled up at the next station I disembarked and tried to find my way through the city's streets to get back to the vision that I had seen. Of course I couldn't find it, but I didn't care.

"I had seen it once and that was enough. The moon was full and bright. I wandered all through the night, finally ending up on the bluff near to my home. I went to Yamate Park and lay down on a bench with a grin on my face and fell asleep. In the morning, I was woken by the sound of children's voices and birds singing. I looked up at the view and in an instant my mind was emptied completely. All that remained was one thought, one firm conviction that I knew was the only truth in the world: Mankind knows nothing.

"I left the Institute the day after my insight. I got together a handful of belongings and took to the road, like one of the poets of old. I wandered the country; I saw the moon rise over the islands of Matsushima and I sat on my hat and wept at the site of the Godaido Shrine. I walked miles every day and I barely ate a thing. I had my insight and that was all the nourishment I needed.

"Three months later my father died. That brought me back down to earth. I returned to the farm immediately in order to attend the funeral. Perhaps I had contributed to his ill health? I don't know. The day after the funeral I helped my mother move to my sister's house in the village, and then I announced to

Mitsuo, our oldest and most trusted employee, that life on the farm was going to change.

"'Mitsuo – I don't want you to prune the trees this year.'

"Mitsuo was already downcast by my father's death. He didn't want more change. I had to plead with him to help.

"'Mitsuo, you have to trust me. No more pruning of the trees. No more pesticides. No more fertilizer. And I want you to open the chicken coop during the day. Let the chickens walk through the vegetable patch. That will be our fertilizer. And I no longer want you to plough the fields. We will sow the seeds directly onto the land and spread the straw from the harvest back over the unploughed fields.'

"I knew that he was completely confused, and I knew that he and the other farmhands thought that I had gone mad, but there was no other choice.

"'Mitsuo, I ask you to do exactly as I request. You must trust me. We are going back to the old farming. We are going back to the farming before the samurai period. We are going back to the Tao. And I will not be moving into the farmhouse. We will all eat there at sunrise and at sunset and we will have tea there during the day to refresh ourselves. All of us together. Everyone who works in the fields and on the mountainside. It will be a place for us all to meet and talk together when it rains, or when it is cold. I will stay in the hut.'

"I do not think I can remember Mitsuo ever questioning my father, but that day I took over the farm he finally could contain himself no longer.

"'But Fumimoto-san, if we do not prune the trees they will die. The branches will become tangled, the sun will not reach the leaves evenly and the trees will become diseased. And if we do not plough the fields … It is unthinkable, Fumimoto-san.'

"The farmhands left the following week. Mitsuo stayed another three seasons, but he was old. Now it is just me, with the occasional help from some of the children from the village. I work hard every day to test whether or not this revelation is true."

The farmer had finished talking. How many minutes had gone by I did not know. He looked up at me and smiled.

"I'm sorry. I have spoken too much. It is a mistake. There is no point in me trying to explain these things with words."

The farmer sighed and looked into the fire.

"If I was a storyteller maybe I could think of a story that would make my point and then you would understand me better."

He fell silent for a moment and then I was heartened to see that the peaceful smile had returned to his face.

"But I am not a storyteller, I am just a simple farmer from Ehime and so the only way I can make my point is through farming. If my insight is correct then all that man does to nature to encourage her to grow is futile and all the practices of modern farming are unnecessary.

"I believe that this is so and I have come back home to my family farm to prove it for all to see, and that is exactly what you find me doing."

Suddenly he stood up. He had a concerned look on his face.

"But let me give you something for those blisters."

I hadn't realized it, but all the time he had been speaking I had been nursing the palms of my hands. The farmer disappeared through the garden door saying that he would be back in a minute. I sat there in silence mulling over all that he had said. I still had so many questions.

It was an extraordinary tale, but most extraordinary of all was the conclusion. The farmer was so sure of his insight that he was prepared to reject everything: progress, science and centuries of farming tradition. He was willing to place them all on the altar of his belief, along with the farm itself, for surely he would lose the farm and his entire livelihood if his insight proved to be wrong.

To be perfectly honest I thought that he was slightly mad. Of course I empathized with him. There was no question about that. After all, I was on a pilgrimage myself because I too had lost faith in the modern world somewhere along the line, so I wasn't hostile to him on principle. It was just that he seemed to be questioning the very foundations of the modern world. He seemed to be questioning both the scientific world-view and the idea of progress. Whole cultures and ways of life were being smashed by the scientific world-view and the forces of progress, and I had long ago given up the idea that a single person could ever stand up to them, let alone achieve anything good on their own.

I felt a great affection for this troubled young man, but I couldn't persuade myself to believe in his vision of farming and of life. It simply could not be possible that all of Western civilization, and indeed eastern civilization, was fundamentally wrong.

How could one man have had an insight into the truth that had somehow escaped everyone else's notice? And even if he did have such an insight, there was no way of actually putting it into practice.

But despite these negative thoughts I still wanted to learn more, just in case, however unlikely

"**H**ere, rub this on your hands."

The farmer had reappeared through the door carrying a handful of leaves.

"I'm sorry but I don't know the English name for this plant."

He squatted down next to me and gave me the leaves. There were four of them. Each one was the size of the palm of my hand.

"Scrunch them up into a ball and squeeze them in your fists. The juices that come out will help to cool your blisters."

The farmer stood up again and watched me, patiently waiting to see what I was going to do. I smiled gratefully at him and did as he instructed. Immediately my hands began to feel less inflamed.

"Thanks very much – that really helps … And thanks so very much for taking the time to talk to me. But can I ask something?"

I paused for a second, trying to think how best I could phrase my question.

"If science is so mistaken, then why does everyone use pesticides and fertilizers nowadays? And how can you possibly grow rice without these things? How do you protect against diseases and pests? And surely there are very good reasons why people plough the soil and use chemicals, otherwise, why else would everyone do it?"

The farmer smiled warmly at me and then shook his head.

"I cannot talk about this any more. You have to see the farm. Only then will you understand."

Outside the golden sun was shining brightly. Just as the farmer had predicted, the mysterious spiders had begun their exodus. All across the silver fields I could see fine threads breaking away and drifting upwards on the summer breeze, carrying their brave passengers off to pastures new. I followed the direction of the wind with my gaze and saw that all the brave spiders were being blown into the commercial farms that surrounded us. They wouldn't last long there, I thought. There would be nothing for them to eat. All the creatures that the spiders preyed upon would already have been killed off with pesticides, and before too long a farm worker would pass through with his sprays and any spiders that were still alive would die an awful death. The spiders had no idea that they were utterly doomed. It was a heart-breaking sight.

I followed the farmer round the side of the farmhouse and we took the path that led past his mud hut and down to the rice fields below. The door to the hut was slightly ajar and as we passed by I was able to glance inside. Lying on the dirt floor was a grass pillow, a blanket and a small piece of candle. I turned back to the path and had to quicken my pace to catch up with the farmer.

"Why don't you sleep in the farmhouse?" I asked when I had caught up.

The farmer turned and stopped for a moment.

"The farmhouse is too big for one man. When more people come to join me then we will all use it as a common room. Besides, I like to live in a simple manner. It makes me more sensitive to nature. If I had electric lights, I would be less aware of night and day. If I had gas-powered heating, I wouldn't notice the changes of the air temperature. All my senses would be blunted."

We continued down the hill. I could not stop myself from shaking my head. Who would be brave enough or mad enough to join this man in his single-minded endeavour to swim against the tide of history? How would he ever persuade anyone to join him in dismantling the practices of the modern world if even his own farmhands had abandoned him?

But just as I was thinking these things, the farmer turned round and smiled at me, and once again I had the disconcerting feeling that he could read my mind.

"They will come. Don't worry. When the farm begins to work, they will come."

He turned away from me again and continued down the path, and as I watched him go a great wave of affection for this gentle, optimistic man washed over me.

But would they come? I was not so sure.

The farmer's rice fields stretched out for several acres in all directions and were bordered in the distance by the rice paddies of the neighbouring commercial farms.

We walked in silence along a carefully mown path that crossed through the growing rice until we were right out in the middle of the fields. Surrounded on all sides by rice plants, I felt finally that I had come to rest on the very bedrock of Japan itself.

"The beginnings of Japanese life!" I exclaimed in delight.

The farmer grinned at me.

"Yes. You are exactly right. From these fields and fields like these, Japanese civilization was born. The rice you see before us now and the winter grains – barley and rye – they are the staples of our land, and the rhythms of the two annual harvests give birth to the rhythms of all Japanese life."

I shielded my eyes with my hand and gazed into the distance. The commercial farms stretched away towards the horizon. For some reason the plants in the commercial fields seemed to stand much taller and their leaves seemed to be much larger. I strained my eyes to make sure my perception was accurate. Without taking my view from the distant fields, I voiced my suspicions out loud.

"Is it just my imagination or are those plants much taller than the ones over here?"

Calmly the farmer responded: "No. It is not your imagination. They are taller. And it is hardly surprising. They are fed on tons of chemical fertilizer and so naturally they shoot up very quickly and waste a lot of energy on extravagant leaves. But that is not the whole story. Look …"

The farmer knelt down and gestured to me to do the same. With the care of someone who was handling a priceless vase he proceeded to examine one of his precious rice plants.

"See, the proof is here. I want my plants to be compact and I want all the energy to be stored in the grains and I want them to be nourished by natural processes: by worms bringing oxygen to the soil, by natural fertilizer made from decaying rice straw and by the microorganisms that exist in my soil but not in the soil of my neighbours' fields."

Cupping the head of a small delicate plant, he studied it.

"My plants each have three or four small leaves, much smaller than those next door. But this year I hope that each plant will yield a hundred grains each. If that happens then they will be yielding more than the outsize plants in my neighbours' fields."

I looked at the delicate grains that rested against the tough palm of the farmer's hand.

"But how can that be?"

"There are many reasons. But let me explain my method then maybe you will understand."

We both rose to our feet.

"In early October, probably next week or a few days after that, I will sow white clover just as we did in the orchard this morning and also I will sow barley …"

I interrupted.

"But how can you sow the barley when you haven't harvested the rice and ploughed the field in preparation?"

The farmer smiled patiently.

"It doesn't matter that the stalks of the rice are still standing and ripening in the late summer sun. It doesn't matter that the fields are never ploughed. None of this matters at all. The tall rice stalks will protect the seeds from the birds, and nature's ploughs, the earthworm and the mole, will till the land for us.

"By the time that I come to harvest the rice, the clover will have grown an inch or two, and then as we walk through the fields harvesting the rice we will trample the sprouting barley seeds into the earth.

"Then, when the harvest is complete, we will thresh and winnow and store the new grains of rice and return the rice straw to the fields. We will lay the straw on top of the sprouting barley and clover to hide the young plants from pests and also to give back nourishment to the earth.

"Then, soon after that, we will sow the rice seeds. They will lie dormant amongst the barley and clover until next spring when they will sprout and give birth to next year's harvest. The chickens will be allowed to wander through the fields and their rich manure will help to decompose the rice and add to the nourishment of the land. All our sowing is complete before the end of the year and we can then return to the orchards above to pick the citrus and persimmons that should now be coming into season.

"All that remains to do is to let in a little water for a week next year. This will drown any weeds but the rice and clover will survive. The clover will turn yellow and look a bit sick, but it is stronger than the weeds and, when the water is removed, it will spring to life again. The clover is the farmer's best friend, for not only does it provide natural fertilizer to the soil, it also suffocates the weeds."

The farmer grinned.

"And that is it. Nature can take care of the rest."

I shook my head in disbelief. I could hear the farmer's words but I didn't know what to think. Even though I could see the proof ripening before my eyes, I could still not quite comprehend that what he was saying was true.

For my whole life I had been made to think of nature and human life in very different ways. Though I did not want to admit it, I had more in common with the commercial farmers and their chemicals, and their way of viewing the world. I thought of nature as a destructive force that had to be fought against in order to prevent the breakdown of civilization. Plants and people both needed to be schooled and educated; they both needed carefully designed environments in which to flourish. They couldn't possibly survive without the aid of modern science.

What is more I wasn't alone. It was the farmer who was the odd one out; it was he and not I who had the strange ideas. No one else in Japan farmed as he did; centuries of trial and error had established hallowed routines of plough and harvest, and besides, there was hardly a farmer left who didn't also use chemicals.

Frustration was welling up within me.

"Why then do people plough? Why then does everyone else in Japan and the developed world use pesticides? Why do they toil away pruning their trees? All over the world people do these things. Are they all wrong? Are they wasting their time? Are you seriously suggesting that centuries of progress in agricultural techniques should be thrown away?"

The farmer was frowning. It was the first time since I had met him that his face had been disturbed by such an expression.

"People think that the modern world has emerged from the chaos of the past; they think that the good comes slowly from the bad. But this is not so.

"In the old days, here on Shikoku Island, people lived happy lives on small farms, eating well. Their houses were made of wood, earth and paper and their clothes were made from cotton and straw. The food they ate grew at their feet and it was the best food in the entire world.

"The winter holiday would last for three months. Farmers even had time to write haikus, to fish and to hunt rabbits in the hills. The harvest was a time of joy and celebration, and people lived healthy lives outdoors under the sun.

"The farmers today work night and day on big machines, laying down chemicals and destroying pests, and in ten years' time almost all the old family farms will be gone. The farmers watch television in the evening or do their accounts. They even have to buy much of their own food from the supermarket.

"Their children leave them for the city where they live tiny, cramped lives, and the farms are swallowed up. Why does this all happen? Most people simply shrug. It is progress towards a better world, they say.

"I don't see that but then maybe I am lucky because I have seen that mankind knows nothing. I may be just a simple farmer, but I know that these people are wrong. I will not follow the crowd, I will follow nature instead."

Since the moment I had first set foot on the farm, I had not seen the farmer so emotional. He turned his head to take in the view of the monotonous fields of the commercial farms, stretching to the horizon.

"When I see my neighbours' fields, I feel an anger that I cannot even begin to express. They are destroying the soil and the ecosystem, and they are destroying their spirits too."

He gazed at me with a look that stung me to my soul. It was a look of accusation.

"How can you call that progress? If such a word is to have any meaning then what we are doing here is progress, for we will not just create healthy rice plants, we will restore the human spirit."

I felt chastened and confused, and yet still I could not let go.

"But there must be good reasons why they do these things? People wouldn't go to all this effort for no reason."

The farmer sighed and looked out over the commercial fields. I knew then that he must have had this battle again and again with people, and I watched as he drew deep on his reserves of patience.

"Once upon a time, when the heroes and gods still walked the earth, rice seeds were blown by the wind directly onto the river's flood plain during the long days of the monsoon rains. The farmer's life was truly carefree and all he did was reap the harvest.

"Then one day he decided that he could improve on this natural method. He began to manufacture earth terraces that could hold the annual floods in place, and he diverted streams and rivers so that he could sow seed and farm on higher ground. And with every experiment his workload gradually increased.

"But these early farmers still stayed close to nature. They saw that when wild rice had had its season its straw and leaves and seeds and husks were all returned to the soil. They knew that after every harvest they too had to give back to the land, but rather than simply return the straw to the field they began to compost it.

"This is an exhausting process, for the compost heap has to be turned by hand with a fork in the hot summer sun. But they toiled away and added this compost, along with manure from the animals that they had domesticated, to the flooded terraces, and ploughed these first fields until they were like the pea soup that they saw on the alluvial plains below.

"And gradually the farmer's work increased again, but still he was not happy. Next he divided the young rice from the old. The young rice was grown in a starter bed and then when it was about seven inches tall it would be transferred by hand into another field where it could grow to maturity until it was ready to be harvested.

"These new fields were works of art. The farmer would spend days on his hands and knees building ridged seed beds. He would light altars on them and make offerings to the gods. He would tidy the ridges and furrows as carefully as a mother arranges a baby's crib. By the time he was finished with all this, his field would look as if it had been made by a master sculptor. The transplant was done by hand, with whole teams of people squatting in the mud for days at a time. From beginning to end every inch of the field was worked over four times – and it is backbreaking work too.

"After the war, the Americans introduced modern chemical agriculture to Japan. People were amazed. By using these chemicals and machines, farmers could grow exactly the same amount of rice as they had grown using the traditional method, but they only had to do half the work. Can you imagine! This was a dream come true. Within a few years, everyone had switched over to the chemical method. But it was not good for the land. Compost and manure were no longer added, there was no need to rotate crops and, very quickly, the structure and quality of the soil deteriorated.

"If you feed people on processed bread and processed meat, it is the same as growing rice plants in this unnatural soil. They will have energy to grow, it is true, but without the diverse plant and animal life, without worms and moles and humus from dead vegetation, the soil will lack all the micronutrients that make a healthy balanced living rice plant. How can you expect someone to be happy on such a diet, living in a tower block in a city, divorced from nature, eating food that is missing so much essential nutrition, surrounded by other people in a similar condition?

"And with the new agriculture fewer people were needed to work the land. It became quicker and easier to lay on the chemicals using farm machinery and so the young people started to drift away. And along with chemicals, ploughing was also introduced to Japan. That is not to say that we had never used the plough before then – even as long ago as the Tokugawa period the land was shallow-ploughed – but it was only after the war that we began to adopt machine ploughing that turns the soil deep down.

"This ploughing is a double-edged sword, like most things in the modern farmer's armoury. For although it is true that ploughing brings air into the soil, it also destroys the natural structure of the soil and it breaks down the great big juicy clods turning them into little crumbs and finally into dust and sand. There is no air in a pile of sand and so it becomes necessary to plough it even more.

"And along with the plough and the chemical fertilizer came the pesticides. The fat, weak plants lost their natural ability to fight off disease and insect damage, and so they became dependent on regular doses of poison. But the residues of these poisons stay in the food and are eaten by us, and the poisons themselves kill everything, including creatures that are essential to the health of the soil.

"But once it has started it is hard to turn back; it would be like taking someone from the heart of Tokyo, someone who drinks coffee and alcohol and eats poor-quality food, and then expecting them to be able to live wild in the countryside. In reality the wild countryside provides for all their needs and it is a healthier place to live. There is no pollution and a million sources of food are available. But the person from Tokyo wouldn't stand a chance."

I shook my head at the thought. What the farmer was saying made so much sense and yet he was almost alone in his beliefs.

"What do your neighbours think of your farming?"

For a second the farmer looked disheartened.

"My neighbours want me to fail. They can only see the bad in what I am doing. They hate me for what I am trying to do because they have become trapped in a nightmare of their own making. Experimental stations, agricultural co-operatives and then farming handbooks: that is the law in the commercial farmer's world – a law that has replaced the rule of nature.

"The co-operatives tell them what to plant when, what combination of fertilizers and pesticides to use, and they tell you all this in the most minute detail, right down to which days of the month you must apply which chemical. This means that the farmer doesn't even have to think about what to do when he gets up in the morning.

"On a preordained day the lorry from the co-operative will arrive to pick up the produce and the farmer will be there, ready and waiting, having packaged up his produce the night before, just as the co-operatives' handbook advised him to do.

"Now imagine if my neighbour dared even to deviate by one iota; imagine what might happen. Perhaps, for example, he thinks one day that he will skip a dose of pesticide. Well, if he does this he might as well just set fire to his fields. The citrus would have a slight discoloration and, consequently, thirty per cent of the fruit would be rejected by the big buyers from Yokohama and Tokyo, and before the snows had come the farmer would be bankrupt.

"I have no bills to pay. I buy no farm machinery or expensive chemicals. If I sell my fruit at a lower price because it does not look as shiny as the other fruit, then it does not matter. I still have enough to live and, what is more, I am twice blessed because I have the honour of feeding the poor people who can't afford the shiny fruit, and I am also feeding them fruit that is far more nutritious.

"Grow a fat, soft rice plant in a flooded field and you get a plant that can be easily attacked by insects and disease. It will look big, but it will always need support from chemical insecticides and fertilizer. Grow a small, sturdy plant in a healthy environment and chemicals are unnecessary. The plant will be filled with the goodness that the human body needs.

"Plough a flooded field by hand or with a tractor and the soil loses its shape and becomes deficient in oxygen; earthworms and microbes die and the earth becomes grainy and lifeless. Then the field has to be ploughed every year.

"Leave the earth to cultivate itself and there is no need for the plough and the tractor. As the soil becomes poorer through ploughing, fertilizer becomes essential, but if fertilizer is used the weeds also grow up strong and so herbicides must also be applied. Return the straw from the harvest to the fields and sow clover with the grain and the soil gets all the nutrition it needs and there is no need for fertilizer or the plough. People meddle with something they don't understand. That is the story of the modern world."

The farmer looked up at me. His face once again wore a gentle smile.

"Do you believe what I tell you, Pilgrim?"

My heart ached to know that what he told me was the truth of the world.

"Yes. I believe you."

The farmer shook his head and stared into the rice plants with a sad look on his face.

"I am glad that you say that, but you have not yet been tested. For now, those are only words."

"It is time I returned to the hillside," said the farmer. "Why not go and drink tea and have a rest in the farmhouse? We can meet again in a couple of hours for some lunch."

I thanked the farmer for all that he had said and bade him farewell, then watched him as he strode through the rice fields and made his steady way back up the hillside, past the farmhouse, through the orchard and onto the wild slopes.

But I didn't feel like a rest. In fact, I wasn't sure what I felt like. All that the farmer had said had profoundly excited my mind.

I took a big lungful of fresh air and, deciding to stretch my legs, I resolved to continue along the mown path through the rice fields until I reached the boundary of his land. I wanted to take a closer look at the commercial fields. The farmer had said so much and I wanted to match what he had said to what I could see with my own eyes.

As I wandered slowly through the rippling acres of rice, a story that I had once read by the great sage Chuang Tzu came into my mind.

Once upon a time, so the story went, there lived a king who owned an enormous prize ox. The King planned to serve this ox at a banquet to celebrate his daughter's wedding, and so he called down to his kitchen and ordered them to send a cook to cut up the beast for the pot.

When a little old man arrived with an ancient carving knife the King was surprised, but because he was a wise man he remained silent and waited for the cook to begin his work.

The little old man walked up to the great beast and, with a slight movement of a shoulder and with the gentle pressing of a knee, the ox fell apart with a whisper.

The King was amazed. "How is it that you can do this?" he asked the old man in disbelief.

The old man shrugged his shoulders and said: "When I first began to cut up oxen I had to think very hard about every stroke. They seemed to be such massive beasts. How long it would take, I thought, how hard I would have to strike. When I finally did start to cut I would hack and hack with all my might to get the job done.

"After three years, I no longer saw the whole animal, I only saw its parts. A steak here, a leg there. I would choose my spot carefully and whack! I would smash through bone and gristle.

"Now, after forty years, I see nothing. My mind is free. My cleaver finds its own way. I touch no bone, I cut no joint. Sometimes there are difficult points. I feel them coming, I breathe, I barely move the blade and *whump* – the beast falls apart like clods of earth. It takes one of the strong young men from the kitchen a whole day to do what I accomplish in a single hour, and at the end his knife is blunt. I have not changed my knife for thirty years."

The King was delighted.

"Your method is the best of all!"

The old cook smiled to himself: "Method?" He shook his head. "I follow nature, beyond all methods."

F ar away on the horizon, great plumes of white cloud climbed towards the heavens, billow stacked upon billow, moving at a gentle summer's pace. Around me on all sides, the golden rice plants rocked and whispered in the breeze. Something in the air spoke of evening rain, of fallen blossoms decorating the lunchtime meal, of the autumn sea and of changes to come.

I had reached the edge of the fields. It had been good to spend the morning with the farmer and his words had made a very deep impression on me. The courage that he displayed in making his stand against the modern, scientific world-view filled me with hope. So strong was the feeling of inspiration that I felt as if a burden that I had been carrying for many years had been lifted suddenly from my shoulders and now I was free to walk through the world with my head held high.

With a light heart I jumped over the narrow irrigation ditch that bordered the rice paddy and, grasping hold of a fence post, I hauled myself up onto the raised ground on the far side of the ditch. The long earthwork divided the farmer's land from that of his neighbour, and before me now lay the endless uniform expanse of the commercial farms. Not a bee buzzed nor a bird sang, and as far as the eye could see there was not one single sign of animal life.

Suddenly, to my amazement, I was confronted by an incredible vision. I shielded my eyes from the sun and looked again. I blinked, thinking that I must have been hallucinating. But the outlandish sight was still there. About twenty yards away, an astronaut appeared to be floating slowly through the commercial field.

Dressed all in white, wearing a hooded, gauze helmet, like the sort that a beekeeper wears, a human being was advancing slowly towards me through the rice plants. His hands were covered by huge, padded white gloves and on his back was strapped an enormous canister. As he walked he rolled from side to side like a deep-sea diver, or a sailor on the deck of an unstable ship. I stood my ground and watched in fascination as the figure struggled along, moving at the speed of an ancient stag beetle, and then suddenly it dawned on me what was going on: he was spraying the crops with poison.

"Hey," I shouted, "stop a minute!"

In my panic I had forgotten all my Japanese. I really didn't want to breathe in lungfuls of dangerous chemicals, and if the wind turned that is exactly what was going to happen.

The strange figure came to an ungainly halt and then very slowly manoeuvred itself round to face me. I was relieved to see that the long tube of the spray was now pointing down towards the ground. I stood frozen to the spot as he began to advance towards me, carving a path through the uniform swathes of the rice plants. Now that he had stopped spraying I found his presence in the field quite surreal.

When he had got to within ten yards he stopped, and the huge white-gloved hands began to struggle ponderously with the helmet. After a minute or so he gave up and the gloves were thrown to the ground; small human hands worked quickly to remove the seals at the neck of the hood, revealing the thin, sweaty face of a young male farm worker.

I smiled keenly, unsure what to say or do, but before I could decide the farm worker grinned back at me and started to shout in Japanese.

I couldn't understand what he was saying but he appeared to harbour no ill intent towards me. He was clearly hot and overexcited by his exertions in the white suit and he was definitely very keen to communicate something.

I shrugged my shoulders in a theatrical fashion.

"I'm sorry. I don't understand Japanese!"

He battled his way closer towards me, kicking his heavy feet up through the fragile rice.

Slapping his head with his gloved left hand and, grinning, he said, "Fumimoto-san is mad!"

I stared at him blankly, not understanding what he meant. Still grinning, he lifted the tip of the spray up into the air and pointed it past me and over towards the far side of the farm, in the direction of an area that I had not yet visited.

"Look. Over there. His farm is dying!"

For a moment the words didn't register but then, when I finally did begin to grasp the implications of what he was saying, all the strength drained away from my limbs.

Through dry lips I said: "What? What do you mean?"

The farm worker was still grinning eagerly.

"Look! There. Up there. All dead."

I turned my head to follow the direction of his arm, and when I saw where he was pointing I felt as if a black shadow had passed over the face of the earth. Suddenly all the exertions of my walk had come home to roost all at once and had fallen on my shoulders at the same time like the blow from a great axe.

On the hillside beyond the farmhouse, in a part of the orchard that I had not yet visited, the skeletal trees were leafless and dead, and in the paddy fields down below there were no golden rice plants rocking in the sunshine; instead there were only diseased brown stalks, motionless as cemetery grass.

I left the farmhand behind me. He was still joyfully proclaiming the farmer's misfortune and grinning like a devil. I could hear him shouting at me in Japanese long after his face was lost behind the earthwork wall.

Breathlessly I strode back down the mown path, unable even to think a single coherent thought. I had to go there and see the evidence for myself. I had to know the worst. After a few minutes I had crossed the golden fields and I found myself confronted by a view as bleak as anything in the land of Sinai.

Every last rice plant was dead. There was not a single stalk ripe for the harvest and higher up on the slopes there was not one living tree left in the orchard. Disease had carried them off, every last one. All that remained of this ancient farm was a scar on the landscape. It was a warning to all who thought they could do without the modern world, that their arrogance would deliver them up only this land of death.

I don't know how long I stood in the fields; such a hammer blow of disappointment robs the mind of normal perception. Finally, I turned my back on the scene of devastation and with a heavy heart I began to make my way back towards the farmhouse.

As I walked I shook my head at my folly. How had I not noticed these fields and orchards before? Perhaps I saw only what I wanted to see. The farmer's idealism and obstinacy were infectious and had blinded me to the truth. I too had wanted to believe that a natural way of farming and a natural way of life were possible. It seemed now that I had to acknowledge to myself that I was so eager to find some reason for optimism in the world that I was prepared to ignore reality. The farmer had delivered up a perfect dream and I had grasped at it as truth. But for all its beauty, it was a dream nonetheless. I had counted some four hundred dead trees in the orchard before I lost heart.

The worst part of it all was that I would now have to face the farmer. And then when I had done that I would have to continue on with my walk, knowing that this strange man did not have any special access to the truth and that his story of a new life was nothing more than a snatch of summer dreams, and in a few more seasons' time there would be nothing left of his farm at all except for a few weed-strewn fields and the acres of overgrown orchards.

I thought of the long road to the monasteries that lay ahead and I thought of the life that I was soon to return to, filled as it was with all its doubts and its bad dreams, and a profound sense of weariness overcame me.

The cold floors and the diet of gruel, mankind at war with itself, the steady arc of progress leading to the giant acres of commercial farms and the frightening phrases of the modern world. I knew now that was the truth of the world and, as I admitted this to myself, I felt my heart sink into the ground.

THE MOON

As I rounded the corner into the farmyard I was jolted from my brooding by a wholly unexpected sight that had the effect of immediately lifting my spirits.

A young woman was standing by the mud hut in the sunlight, holding a basket of bright yellow flowers. She had a beautiful pale face and long black hair that was tied in tresses down her back, and she was wearing a pale blue kimono. She looked just like one of the pretty country girls that are depicted in the classical prints.

Behind her, at the main entrance to the farmyard, stood a magnificent snow-white mare, hitched to a trap. Standing next to the trap was a stout young man, clearly the driver, and sitting on the passenger seat was an austere-looking elderly woman draped in a shawl, her arms folded neatly on her lap.

Only the snow-white horse had noticed me. She watched me through her solemn, pink-rimmed eyes, jerkily raising her right foreleg and flicking her mane.

I was just about to step out of the trees and into the farmyard when the farmer, carrying a large box of fruit and vegetables, suddenly appeared through the farmhouse door. The sight of him instantly made me feel ashamed of my thoughts of only moments before.

The peaceful labour of the farm, the constant fresh air and sunshine, his frugality, but above all the purity of his soul gave him a kind of aura of vitality that instantly worked to restore my faith. Confused, I stayed back, half hidden behind the fronds of a citrus tree.

I watched in fascination as he presented the box to the young woman, laying it at her feet. They were both smiling warmly and he was gently explaining something to her. It was a touching scene completely out of kilter with my mood of despair, and it occurred to me that perhaps I was wrong; perhaps a portion of the farm was bound to die when such a revolution occurred. After all, the farmer was trying something never before attempted. He was pioneering a new way of living with nature; what it depended on for success, more than anything else, was the faith to persevere against setbacks. My own faith had been tested and I had failed.

Just then the young woman noticed me. Without moving at all, she lowered her dark eyes and whispered quickly to the farmer. I must have been a most unexpected sight. I doubt that many foreigners had ever been seen coming in from the fields of Ehime before. The farmer spun round urgently, but when he saw me he laughed and hailed me in his gentle voice.

"Aha! Pilgrim! It is you! You are frightening my guests!"

I stepped out of the trees and into the farmyard and a wave of affection for the farmer filled my heart. He had turned back to the young woman and was clearly explaining to her who I was and that she should not worry. I walked over to join them. As I crossed the yard I felt the old woman's eyes following my every move.

The farmer had changed his clothes since I had last seen him. He had on a clean blue-cotton work shirt and an unblemished pair of cloth shoes. His tanned muscle-bound forearms were waving around excitedly as he spoke first in English then in Japanese.

"James! Please, I would like you to meet Masumi. She is from the village down by the shores of the Inland Sea."

I bowed low. Now that I was close to the young woman I could see how strikingly beautiful she was. Her skin was completely perfect and her crimson lips glowed with good health. I was so surprised by her beauty after weeks of rugged countryside that I blushed like a schoolboy, and it was only the coaxing of her sympathetic gaze and kind smile that made me recover my senses.

"And this is her mother, Madam Kimiko," said the farmer.

Tearing myself away from the gaze of the young woman, I turned to face the old lady across the yard and bowed low. She looked on unmoved.

The farmer was talking again. I had not seen him like this before. The presence of the young woman had transformed him. All his energy and attention seemed to be directed towards her. I could not help chuckling to myself and noting that, for all his single-mindedness, even he wasn't immune to human beauty.

"Masumi and Madam Kimiko visit every week and I give them the best fruits and vegetables from the orchard. Today they will have some pomegranates and some apples."

His hands were in the box, sorting through the contents.

"The shopkeeper in Fumimoto tells me that my apples taste just like sherbet. They fizz on the tongue when you bite into them."

Like a magician he held up an apple, and then a second later it had turned into an orange, then a pomegranate. The young woman smiled at him affectionately, and then she turned her soft, intelligent eyes onto me and to my great surprise she spoke to me in English. Her voice was warm and kind.

"Do you like it here on the farm?"

Once I had recovered from the shock I stammered a reply.

"Yes … Yes, it's a lovely place."

The farmer watched us silently and with interest. The young woman hardly moved, but there was a maturity and wisdom in her thoughtful eyes that went far beyond her years.

"Yes. It's very peaceful here."

Suddenly, the farmer stood up again.

"James, I must go up to the orchard and pick some choice vegetables. Perhaps you could show Masumi and her mother the spiders' webs. I think that they would like to see them. I will join you in a moment."

Whilst the farmer disappeared up the hillside into the trees, I helped the old lady down from the trap and led her and her daughter through the farmhouse and out into the back garden where the view of the fields below was at its best.

I hadn't forgotten about my crushing discovery of only minutes before, but the young woman was so captivating that it was only when we stepped into the garden and I noticed out of the corner of my eye the black lands of failed rice and the slopes of dead and dying trees that the sense of despair returned.

The dead lands were not easily visible from the back of the farmhouse. That must have been why I hadn't noticed them earlier that morning. But instead of pointing out the dead lands, I found myself feeling protective towards the farmer and his dream – I don't know why. I pointed the young woman and her mother in the opposite direction. I didn't want anyone to know the truth until I had first confronted the farmer. But they were staring in wonder at the dazzling, shimmering, silver-clad fields that flashed like a giant mirror in the down below. Even the old lady could not suppress her awe and, for a second, the expression on her face became one of almost childlike joy.

Standing in the garden at the back of the farmhouse I told the story of the spiders' mysterious appearance and even more mysterious disappearance to the young woman, and in turn she translated my explanation for her mother. By now the old lady had regained her composure and severity and, as she listened to her daughter, a look of disdain marked her ancient features.

I explained how no one knows where the spiders come from or where they go, and I explained that they were lucky to see such a sight today because since people had started to use pesticides almost all such natural cycles had been destroyed.

The young woman listened with interest until after a few minutes she stopped translating for her mother and looked at me directly. Her mouth had the first hints of a knowing smile.

"How do you know all these things?"

I blushed.

"The farmer taught me. I did not know them until this morning."

She studied my face for a moment with her beautiful eyes and then her expression slowly turned from humour to anxiety.

"So you believe what he says about the world and nature? Do you believe also in what he says about ploughing and chemicals? Do you believe then that the farm will work?"

It was the first time that I had seen beyond the calm composed face and into the mind of this woman, and for whatever reason she clearly cared a great deal about the fate of the farmer and his work.

For a moment I was too confused to answer. I thought of the dead trees and the black field, but then I thought too of the golden rice plants and the magical orchard with its profusion of life, and then I thought of the farmer and the extraordinary power of his will.

"Yes. It will work."

She lowered her eyes. She was so completely in control of even her smallest gestures that her body language provided no insight into her real thoughts.

Nevertheless, I sensed that she seemed somehow comforted by my answer, although it was impossible to know for sure.

We stood in silence for a minute or so, contemplating the wonderful natural scene, until finally the old lady muttered something in Japanese.

Masumi turned to me and said with a kind smile: "It is time for us to return home now. Thank you very much for showing us this beautiful sight."

As we stepped back into the farmyard the farmer appeared down the path from the orchard, carrying a bamboo box filled to the brim with fresh vegetables of every kind. He was smiling happily and he greeted the two women in Japanese before passing the box to the driver who loaded it onto the trap.

I said goodbye to the young woman and she wished me a safe journey home and then I lingered in the doorway of the farmhouse, not wanting to get in the way of the farmer's farewells. The driver helped the old lady back up into the trap whilst the farmer and the young woman stood in the centre of the farmyard saying their goodbyes.

As I stood in the doorway watching the young couple talk, the truth of the situation suddenly revealed itself to me in a blinding flash and I felt foolish for not having understood it sooner. The farmer and the young woman were deeply in love.

They were standing facing each other, yet they were closer together than two people who were just friends would ever stand. I could not hear what they were saying but it did not matter for in such situations words only serve to obscure the truth.

What they really thought and felt was there for all to see. Their bodies yearned to be together. The farmer's open hands were frozen in front of him, as if he wanted only to clutch her by the waist and draw her to him, whilst her head was bowed as if she longed more than life itself to lie upon his chest.

Their lips must have moved, but all I could see were two motionless statues forever unable to consummate their love.

So strong was the sense of passion and intimacy that I felt forced to avert my gaze altogether, as if I was staring directly at the sun. I thought of the line from the poet Issa who described the parting of two lovers as being more painful than a fingernail being pulled from a finger.

As soon as I sat down by the fire, my thoughts took a very bleak turn. The folly of the farmer's revolution against the modern world seemed suddenly all the more enormous, for I was sure now that the success of the farm was somehow linked to his prospects of living a happy life with the young woman.

Of course it was only my suspicion, but I knew enough about Japanese life to believe that this was the case and besides, my instincts told me that I was right. I recalled the anxiety with which the young woman had asked me for my opinion on the chances of the farm's success, and I recalled also the steely and suspicious gaze of the old lady who had overseen the young woman's trip.

For the first time I was angry with the farmer. I was angry with him because I did not want to see someone who was plainly so good suffer such a tragic fate. His attempt to live a truer life now seemed cavalier.

It was one thing to risk his own livelihood in pursuit of a noble dream, but to squander the love of this beautiful woman as well was utter madness, particularly as he was clearly every bit as much in love with her as she was with him.

Now that heartbreak seemed to be the likely outcome of his radical experiments, I wanted to beg him to stop. The worst thing of all was that it was the farmer's very purity of spirit that had got him into this predicament. He believed that he had been shown the way to the truth and he was prepared to make no compromises at all to get there. I shook my head in frustration. I needed to talk to him straight away and the first thing I had to know was the truth behind the dead fields and trees.

When the farmer finally came inside he was clearly troubled and deeply preoccupied with his own thoughts. He smiled at me, but his brow remained furrowed and as he arranged the vegetables for lunch I thought I heard him sigh more than once. Seeing him like this I once again felt unable to challenge him. I didn't want to heap more pain upon his head.

Instead I offered to help him prepare lunch. He refused my offer of help and instead he asked me to relax and enjoy the peace of the day. I sat back to sip my tea and tried to make myself as unobtrusive as possible. I felt like a dog that senses that his master is troubled and so sits quietly in the corner until the dark mood passes.

The farmer finished cooking and handed me a bowl of delicious food and then sat down himself and began to eat. He seemed a little happier now and so I could contain myself no longer, but when I finally opened my mouth I spoke almost in a whisper, as if half hoping that he wouldn't hear what I had to say.

"I ran into one of the neighbours this morning," I began.

The farmer didn't look up. He continued to chew his gruel and study the smouldering embers in the fire grate.

I pressed on.

"He said that last year the rice and barley harvests were down. That they were lower than before, when your father had been in charge."

I felt as if I was plunging a dagger into the farmer's heart and then turning it one way and then the other.

"And so I went to look myself and I counted more than four hundred dead trees on the northern slopes and I saw the rotten fields …"

He stopped chewing and at that moment I wished that there had been someone else in the room, someone with whom I could share the burden of making these terrible accusations. The farmer's face was impassive. He glanced up from his food and looked me in the eye.

"And he is right."

In that one awful instant that it took him to utter those words, my heart sank. How could it be? How could he be telling me that his natural method was the best when all along he had known that it was failing?

"And he said that your farming doesn't work."

The farmer sighed and put down his bowl and then spoke again.

"And do you believe him?"

"I don't know …"

I saw his chest rise and fall. He shook his head in disappointment and then summoned the energy to try to explain.

"When nature is trained and tampered with over generations it becomes hard to return it to its proper course. The reason that you see those dead trees is because the first year I did what I thought was natural. I left the orchard to its own devices. I did no pruning and I barely set foot under the trees. The branches became tangled, branch overlapped branch and some leaves were cast into shadow where they became infected or were attacked by insects. Many trees died.

"The same happened down in the fields. I left the rice plants to their own devices thinking that without interference they would be free to grow up tough and hardy. But much of the rice crop was too addicted to the chemicals and it had forgotten how to cope without the nitrogen and phosphates, and its natural defences that had been made unnecessary by the years of pesticides had broken down …"

He leant forward and put another small piece of wood on the summer fire.

"I was foolish. I thought that I could return this farm to its natural state overnight. Of course it was never going to be that easy, no more than one can quickly restore a human being who is dependent on all the crutches and supports of modern urban civilization to natural health."

He looked up at me again and I could see in his eyes a sincere desire to convince me.

"Nature is so sturdy and yet she is so delicate. The trees in the orchard can survive frost and floods and battery by wild storms. The bough of a citrus tree is as strong and unbreakable as a leather whip. Can the wind and rain hurt a whip? No. But if a man goes into the orchard with a pair of scissors and chooses a young tree and cuts down a single bud from that tree, then that alone will be enough to change the course of the life of the whole plant. That bough will grow short and will be buried by the other limbs of the tree.

It will fall into shadow and it will become the prey of insects and disease. One day the disease may grow to take over the whole tree. And so because one year we made just one cut, we are obliged forever more to trim and cut all the branches to compensate and try to return the tree to its natural state. Surely, it is better never to cut at all?"

I was so confused. I didn't know whether to believe what he was saying or not. All I knew was that his farm appeared to be on the brink of total failure.

"But will the farm survive? Can you ever bring it back in line with nature?"

"The first year was bad. I lost three hundred trees, half an acre of rice and half an acre of barley. The second year it was much worse. But last year was only as bad as the first year. I lost three hundred more trees in the northern end of the farm and rice blast carried off half an acre, but some of the trees that almost died in the first year have now begun to return to full health and these new trees are so strong and vigorous you would be amazed to see them. After three years I have studied the natural shape so carefully that I can now keep my pruning to the minimum and next year I will hardly have to prune at all."

I inhaled deeply in shock. Over one thousand trees destroyed. This ancient orchard, tended by hand since the days of the samurai, decimated in three years. And more than an acre and a half of rice and barley lost to disease that could be prevented so easily with a regular dose of poison. I shook my head in awe at the destruction.

"But what if the harvest is down again next year? I am sorry to ask you this, but what if you still haven't got it right? What if the farm shrinks even further? How will you survive?"

"That won't happen, but even if it did I need little to survive. I gave away all the family savings as alms for the poor. I sold all the farm machinery and gave the profit away too. Nature will provide for me, she will fill my belly and the barn as well. No one comes to the farm to rob me, for I have nothing. It is the commercial farmers who need money. Their plants are addicted to the expensive chemicals. They need machinery and fuel and spare parts. I need only my own good health."

As he spoke I thought of Masumi the young woman, waiting patiently. I had to struggle to suppress my rising sense of disbelief at this gentle man's seeming inability to engage with the modern world, but when I thought of her I could suppress my horror no longer. Slowly and deliberately, I framed my question. Although I feared his answer, I had to know the truth.

"Please, forgive me for asking, but who is Masumi and why does she really come every week?"

For the first time since I'd met him, the farmer looked embarrassed and a blush coloured his ruddy cheeks.

"Masumi and I grew up together in the village and used to play in the meadows and woods. She was my childhood sweetheart …"

He paused and stared at his hands on his lap.

"Masumi was engaged to be married to a rich young man, but he died in the war…"

He looked up at me and for the first and only time I sensed that he was seeking my understanding in a different way.

"Next spring, just after the barley harvest, we plan to marry. Her father was a rich merchant. He is dead now, but her mother and brothers will only allow the marriage to go ahead if the farm is successful and I have prospects. You see, they do not understand. They regard what I am doing as madness and so they withhold their permission but I am confident that by next spring I will be able to show them that they are wrong."

I could scarcely believe my ears. It was all far worse than I had feared. Although I had only known this man for a few hours, I felt completely bound up in his fate.

"But, Fumimoto-san, you can't do this. You can't go on like this. Why not go to the agricultural co-operative and ask for some pesticide, just for this one year at least? Let someone else follow your dream, or do it in some years' time when you are married and have a family and the farm is prosperous. You will be wealthy then and you can devote a small corner of the land to experiments."

The farmer interrupted my desperate pleadings.

"James, that would never work. I would become a different person if I did what you advised. In life you can either choose to follow your heart or not. There is no middle way. You cannot follow your heart a little bit, just in the evenings, or only at the weekends.

"It is like the women who dye the clothes in the village. Every day they wash the cotton in the vats of blue dye, and after ten years their hands are stained for ever. If I did what you say and became a commercial farmer, I would be rich and prosperous, maybe, but I would for ever more be a commercial farmer. I would forget the insight that I have had and no one would ever know that all mankind's ideas of progress are mistaken and that the world doesn't have to be like this."

He paused again and looked up at the ceiling and sighed.

"Sometimes I lie awake at night in the mud hut, with only the moon as my companion, and I wonder to myself. If it were possible to pass this cup to someone else then maybe I would."

He turned his face to me again and his eyes were

burning with passion. He raised the palms of his hands to the heavens.

"But look around! There is no one else – not on this farm, not in Yokohama, not even in the whole of Japan, not even perhaps in the world. So it falls on me to do it. Humanity must learn that it knows nothing, or its arrogance will only bring more death and destruction and unhappiness. And words alone will never convince people so I must demonstrate that this is true and the only way I can do this is through farming ..."

We fell into silence again.

Finally, I said: "But how can you bear to carry on, with the risk of losing her hanging over your head? Doesn't your rational mind tell you that this is madness?"

"James, it is often the fate of lovers that they have to suffer difficult trials. I simply think that Masumi and myself are no different. And you are right, my rational mind does panic and it does try to take control of my life, but that is not the way.

"I think of the tale of the brave archer Yoichi who was challenged to shoot a single fan suspended over a boat drifting offshore. He drew back the string and took aim with his mind, but his eyes watered and his fingers shook. Luckily, he was wise, he let his heart, not his mind, take aim and loose the arrow, and he hit his mark.

"So you are right: sometimes, my mind tries to deceive me and tell me there are other ways, but in my heart I know this is not so. And if you do not do what you know in your heart of hearts to be right, then all else is lost, all else will unravel.

"If I take one step back down the road from which I have turned, my heart will shrivel up into dust and in a single night I will become like an old man. I have seen the truth of the world and now I can never betray it. If I do I will lose my spirit itself and if that happens I will also lose Masumi …"

I shook my head in wonder. I was now so confused that I could not even recognize the emotions I was feeling. Was it despair? Or was it hope? Or was it simply incredulity at the courage of the farmer who was making this lonely, foolhardy stand against the modern scientific world and the arrogance of foolish and childish mankind?

The farmer was looking at me with pity.

"Have you forgotten that you have also seen the healthy orchard and that you have walked amongst the sturdy rice plants that are ripening in the fields below? You are like a child who has lost both his parents and doesn't know what to believe. Or like the lamb who has been separated from the flock and doesn't know where to turn.

"I tell you that, within seven years, even the barren field that we worked this morning will bring forth great fruit and not one drop of poison will have sullied its earth. This farm will be reborn. The summer is on its way. You must have faith."

"And what about Masumi?"

"Masumi is dearer to me than all the world. I will never allow her to become a lonely spinster. We will marry next year when the cherry blossoms are in full bloom. The seven herbs of spring will adorn her bridal gown and the children from the village will be her bridesmaids."

He rose to his feet.

"But it is time now for me to go back out. One man's life on earth is nothing more than an echo resounding through the mountains and off into the empty sky. If I am to leave my mark here so that others can find inspiration, then I must work hard day and night. Will you join me or not?"

I looked down at my hands. Miraculously, the blisters seemed to have healed completely.

"Yes. Even if I can't use the scythe any more, I can at least walk behind you and sow the seeds."

I stood up and followed the farmer through the door and out into the warm embrace of the late afternoon sun.

There once was an Emperor who owned a night-coloured pearl. No one who had asked had ever been allowed to see this pearl and even the Emperor himself had never laid eyes on it, for it was such an ancient heirloom that it was kept locked away in a box. But the Emperor often explained that the smooth-running of the empire depended entirely upon the night-coloured pearl's safekeeping.

One day the Emperor went wandering to the north over the cold mountains and across the dark sea and when he got to the edge of the world, he looked over to see what lay beyond.

When he returned home he realized that the night-coloured pearl had gone. The people, who had previously been as honest as the deer in the woods, had become greedy and unruly. The trustworthy men now knew that there was a value to their trustworthiness and the virtuous men, who previously had been as meek as the lambs in the fields, knew that they were virtuous and secretly they puffed up their chests.

The Emperor shook his head in despair. The whole empire was beginning to crumble. "I should never have gone to look over the edge of the world. I must find the night-coloured pearl."

First, he sent out scientists to find it. They invented microscopes and telescopes and all sorts of machines, but the more they looked, the bigger the world became. No telescope could see far enough and no microscope could see small enough; there was always something further away or something smaller to see. Finally, they threw up their hands in despair and sighed, "this way will never work."

So the Emperor turned to the philosophers, but the more they thought and argued the more confused they all became.

Finally, in desperation, he turned to his generals. "You have to help me. Go into our neighbours' lands and do whatever you have to do to bring me back the night-coloured pearl."

Soon there were war horses and soldiers camped in the suburbs, and slaves marched in chains through the streets.

The Emperor retired to bed in despair but when he fell asleep he had a dream and in the dream he saw a small child playing in a meadow. The Emperor walked out into the field and the child stopped her game and spoke.

"Why do you look for it when it cannot be seen? Why do you listen for it when it cannot be heard? Why do you reach for it when it can never be grasped? If you approach it, it will recede. If you draw away from it, it will come. Softly it flows, like water, and yet it destroys the hardest things. It dwells in the low places that people disdain and all the rivers of the world pour into it. It does not stand in front of the crowd, it sits behind. It does not shout out loud from rooftops, it whispers in the dead of night."

On hearing these words the Emperor became even more desperate.

He fell to his knees before the child and begged: "But I have to have the night-coloured pearl. I want it more than life itself."

The child looked at the Emperor very solemnly.

"Move as cautiously as someone crossing a tightrope over a ravine. Be as courteous as a guest in a stranger's house and as alert as a spy in an enemy camp. Be as fragile as melting ice and malleable as a lump of clay. Be as clear and still as a glass of water. But never, ever, try to possess the night-coloured pearl."

The Emperor woke up in terror. He was exhausted and he had gone past the point of despair. He sank back into his bed in a fever and remembered his dream, and then he realized that he would never find the night-coloured pearl.

Finally, his mind cleared and even despair had left him and there, in the middle of nothingness, was the night-coloured pearl.

The Emperor shut his eyes and smiled to himself.

"Nothingness, whom I never bothered to ask for help, all along had the night-coloured pearl."

And so the following morning we parted company. We had worked till late in the fields the night before and the moon was up as we made our slow way back to the farmhouse. After dinner I had collapsed exhausted into my bed by the fire. I was not used to farm work, but more exhausting than the farm work itself had been the experiences of the day.

The farmer's entire life and work had the effect of opening up great new vistas to me that left me filled with hope but which also left me feeling overwhelmed from the effort of trying to understand everything I was seeing.

The next morning after breakfast, the farmer gave me back my shirt. It was shining white like the robes of a king. He handed me some rice wrapped in a banana leaf and filled my water bottle with fresh water. I gathered together my handful of belongings and set about tidying my bedclothes. I folded up the blue work shirt that he had lent me and arranged the slippers neatly next to the grass pillow.

I stepped into the farmyard for the last time to find the farmer talking quietly to an old man who was also dressed in the straw shoes and blue-cotton work clothes of the traditional farmer. A brown farm horse was tied to the wooden gate. When the farmer saw me he broke off from his conversation and, looking around at the beautiful day, he smiled.

"It is a fine morning for a departure. Even the last spiders have decided to go."

He turned to the old man and said something in Japanese and then ushered me over.

"Come and meet Mitsuo. He has come up this morning to help me with some delicate work. I think that I am skilled in the orchard but, if I watch Mitsuo for even one minute, I always learn something new."

Whilst I bowed to the old man and muttered a few phrases in my halting Japanese, the farmer walked over and unhitched the horse from the post and led it back over.

"There are hundreds of crossroads in the wood. A stranger like you will definitely go astray – but I think you already know that. This horse knows the way. He will lead you safely to the village where you can rejoin your path. When you reach the first house, take him by the bridle, turn him round and pat him on the flank and he will come back here."

He adjusted the reins and tightened the saddle belt under the horse's belly and then turned to me for one last time.

"You are sure you won't stay? Perhaps you should rest for one more day? You could join us in the orchard. It is not such hard work as out in the fields. Or you could just stretch your legs in the wood."

I smiled and shook my head.

"Yes. I'm sure. But thank you. It's time I pressed on. Besides, I would only slow you two down."

"You are too hard on yourself! You saved me many hours of work. I only hope that one day you will come back here and see the fruits of your labour."

I smiled in gratitude as I struggled to suppress a tear. Forgetting the customs of rural Japan I stepped up to the farmer and hugged him warmly and grasped his right hand firmly in my own.

"Thank you for all your hospitality. I'm so grateful to you for sharing this time with me. I cannot find the words."

The farmer placed his hand on my shoulder and smiled.

"There is no need for words."

He helped me up into the saddle and then, taking the horse by the bridle, he led us to the farmyard gate and patted the horse on its flank.

"Farewell, Pilgrim. Until we meet again!"

And so it was on horseback that I finally left this marvellous place. As I gently swayed from side to side, enjoying the rocking motion of the horse's patient steps, I looked back up towards the top of the orchard to where I had first entered this strange world, only one day and a lifetime before, and in the distance I could see the orange glow of the citrus fruits hiding in the healthy trees.

Enjoying the experience of being a passenger, I soaked up the morning sun. The track climbed the hill and bent slowly round the top of the farm before plunging back into the wooded slopes above, but before we disappeared into the shade of the trees I turned to look down the hill one last time.

I could see the farmer and Mitsuo wending their quiet way through the misty orchard, two shepherds amongst their ever-trusting flock. As they walked they stopped and touched the trunks of the trees as if they were patting the flanks of their favourite horses. They reached up and pulled upon the outstretched boughs, as if they were shaking hands with old friends. I watched the farmer bend down and forage amongst the ground cover, inspecting leaves and searching for the friendly pests that he prized so highly and holding them up to show Mitsuo before replacing them on the same leaves from which he had just taken them.

The two men didn't seem to be in a hurry. They looked like connoisseurs of some sort, as indeed they were, taking a leisurely stroll through a living art gallery.

Would the seed of a new kind of life, scattered here by the wind, take hold? If it were a question of purity of heart and purpose then I did not doubt it. The farmer was relying on his belief that the modern world was quite wrong and that mankind knew little about the true workings of nature. Only time would reveal if this conviction was enough.

All I could do was offer my friends one last silent prayer as the horse carried me through the low-hanging branches and slipped into the shadows of the wood. Was he a genius or was he a madman? And would I ever see him again? A verse of Basho floated into my mind and I bowed my head to its mournful power:

Separated we shall be
Forever, my friend,
Like the wild geese
Lost in the clouds.

I dearly hoped it would not be so but even if it were I was not leaving empty-handed, for although at the time I only partially realized it, I was carrying away with me back to Europe something almost as precious as friendship itself: the seeds of a new life.

As I finally lost sight of the farm and settled back into the rocking motion of the horse's gait, I realized that I no longer needed to continue my pilgrimage and that it was time now to head for home.

THE STARS ABOVE

ABOVE

Days and months are milestones of eternity, so are the years that pass us by.

It is hard to explain the transformation that had been wrought within me by going to Japan but on my return home I found that above all else I now wanted to work with people. A new sense of optimism had taken hold of me, a sense of optimism that I was desperate to communicate to others. I had rediscovered hope and I now knew that the world was not always as gloomy as it sometimes seemed.

I got a job as a teacher in a school, a job that I did for seven years. A schoolteacher's life is busy and I had very little time to think about farming. To tell the truth, I was young and I was experiencing so many new things all the time and I was so full of the impatience and forgetfulness of youth that I didn't realize the extent to which this change in my outlook on life was the natural flowering of a seed that had been planted during those twenty-four hours spent on a hillside in Japan.

Instead, I set my experiences with the farmer aside and got on with my life. All I knew was that the darkest days had finally passed and that my mood had changed for the better, but in my ignorance I put this down to fresh air and foreign travel in general and not specifically to my experiences at the farm.

As soon as I set foot on English soil again I instantly became caught up in all the normal complications of life that I had been unable to engage in for the past few years. Where was I going to live? What was I going to do with my life? How was I going to earn a living? Some of my friends had already established themselves in their careers and I needed to get going with mine. It was time to start afresh on the road of life.

During that first year after my return from Japan, if I did ever think of the farmer I thought of him as a dreamer, engaged in a brave but probably hopeless struggle against the problems of the world. But mostly, I didn't think about him at all. I was simply far too busy.

It turned out that teaching was a good choice of career. I felt that I could contribute to the world by having a positive influence on my young students. I taught history and occasionally, when the syllabus permitted, I taught lessons on Japanese poetry.

Life was good but although I was more optimistic than I had been prior to my departure for Japan, deep down I could still never entirely throw off the same old feeling of unease, the feeling of unease that had prompted my original journey.

For what kind of world would the children I taught actually inherit? And what about their peers all around the world? What about the less fortunate children who woke every day into the grim realities of supposedly positive words like "globalization" and "growth"?

And as the years went by I found myself wondering more and more about what might have happened to my friend.

It was in the classroom that memories of the farmer returned most often. Children have a special facility for asking awkward questions and it is the teacher's lot that he or she has to learn how to answer them. Every teacher finds their own way to respond to such questions as: "If humanity is meant to be progressing then why are we destroying the world around us?" or: "Why are some people starving to death when we have so much food?" or: "If science and technology are meant to improve the world, why is it more dangerous than ever?"

It was at times like this that I sometimes found myself thinking of the farmer and his life, and slowly but surely questions of my own began to work away at the back of my mind. Could he have actually done it? Could he have succeeded or was the farm now nothing more than a stretch of overgrown, weed-covered fields? And was he now a married man, or had the barley harvest failed the following spring?

I wanted to tell the children about the farmer and to urge them not to lose faith in the world. I wanted to explain that there were other ways of living; that the farmer had chosen to walk one of these paths and it had brought him harmony and happiness.

But, as I didn't know if he had succeeded or not, I couldn't in good conscience hold him up as an example of a new life. As it was, his existence would have sounded like something out of a fairy tale to them and, until I knew one way or another if he had succeeded, I would have to regard his struggle as nothing more than a dream.

But as time went by I knew that it was becoming increasingly important for me to learn what had become of him. I contemplated going back there, to find out what had happened. But then I always stopped myself – it would simply be too much for me to bear to find out that this brave man's efforts had been in vain and that the place where I had spent that magical period of time no longer existed at all. I grew to dread the possibility that a commercial farm now stood in its place with its monotonous acres of machine-harvested rice and parade-ground ranks of doctored trees; and that the farmer too had long departed, forced to work with machines on another farm, or worse still to find work in the city itself.

In any case, I was at the beginning of my career and I was far too busy to go and find out what had happened over the ensuing years. Besides, as long as I didn't know the truth, I could at least still hope.

As is the way with life I found myself slowly climbing the ladder of my chosen career and as every year passed I took on more responsibility and began to grow into a middle-aged man. Life continued in this fashion until at the end of my seventh year at the school I was offered a sabbatical, which I duly accepted. I had some savings and I hadn't been abroad for many years so I had a great desire to breathe a little pure air. I decided that it would be a good time to return to Japan. Without any preconceived notion beyond that, I struck out again for the ancient Buddhist pilgrimage trail around the Island of Shikoku where I had had the extraordinary experience all those years before.

The country had changed. As soon as I set foot in Tokyo I could see and hear and feel the stirrings of progress all around.

There were many more cars on the streets of the capital and many more people were wearing Western clothes. There were advertising billboards tempting people to buy white goods and new household products, and everywhere I turned traditional buildings were being pulled down and replaced by new structures made from concrete and steel.

In the shops, people could buy things that they would never have thought of owning before: gramophones, vacuum cleaners and even leather armchairs, which was especially strange as Japanese people still, almost without exception, sat on the floor on Tatami mats.

I recognized too that a new Western scale of values was being used by the average Japanese man or woman. People wanted to buy things because they were new and not because they needed them.

Outwardly at least, Japan appeared to be striding happily into a future of Western-style industrialization. The government, which had always in the past been so scornful of the materialism of Western culture, now seemed to have decided actually to hold it up for admiration.

I knew that things weren't that simple of course. The catastrophic shock that had been dealt to the foundations of the old order by the dropping of the atom bombs, combined with the presence of the victors, living as an occupying force, making laws and refashioning society, had destroyed a lot of the Japanese people's ancient self-confidence.

The whole place left me feeling bewildered. So many good things were being jettisoned as part of the general clearing out of the old samurai culture and so much bad seemed to be coming into Japan. And of all the things that I held dear about Western society and that I thought would be most worthy of export, none of them seemed to have made their presence felt at all.

When I finally reached Shikoku on my third day in the country I was dizzy with all the changes and all the more eager to get out into the tranquillity of the remote countryside.

My plan was somehow to make my way to the little village of Fumimoto and from there ask directions to the farm. After that, whether the farm existed or not and whether or not I was reunited with my old friend, I would return to the pilgrims' trail and finish the walk that I had begun all those years ago.

I had assumed that I would have to catch a train to the southern end of the island and then make my way from there, but I found instead that there was now a sophisticated bus network connecting all the outlying regions of the island and that I could catch a bus the following morning and be at my destination by late afternoon. How times had changed: ten years ago, this journey alone would have taken at least three days.

Throughout the night in Matsuyama I was filled with a growing sense of foreboding. What if the farm was no longer there? Whilst this possibility had remained in the abstract I had been able to keep the potential consequences of this eventuality from my thoughts, but now that I was actually going to discover the truth the following day, I became agitated beyond belief and was unable to sleep the whole night long.

Without my realizing it, over the years the farmer's struggle had somehow gained a great personal significance for me. As long as I knew that there might be one person left in the world who had successfully demonstrated that there was another, better way of living then I could still have hope. But if it now transpired that the farmer and his farm had vanished like a snatch of summer dreams and that there was finally nothing left for me in this world other than the bleak mantras of science and progress, my spirit would be shattered into a thousand pieces.

I seriously contemplated turning back and returning to Europe on the next flight just so that I could maintain my state of ignorance, but when the first slivers of grey light appeared at the edges of the curtains in my little hotel bedroom I realized that I had no choice but to go on. I went to the bus station and got on the bus and found myself a seat at the back by the window where I dozed my way through the first hours of the new day.

By late afternoon we were driving through scenery that I should have recognized from before for we were now approaching Fumimoto and this was the land that I had patiently trodden on foot. But the small farms had almost all disappeared – replaced instead by gigantic acres of machine-farmed land. The hamlets were quieter and some of them even had a noticeably sad air about them. There were fewer children running in the meadows, fewer dogs and horses in the streets everywhere I looked, and there were machines doing the work of men. The workforce itself had been decimated.

I got off the bus at Fumimoto and was struck by the calm of the place. When I had first entered the village on horseback, fresh from the farm all those years ago, it had been buzzing with life, but now it appeared empty and desolate. There were one or two people in the little main street, but none of them seemed to want to meet my gaze.

I took this all to be a very bad omen and as I started to get my bearings a feeling of queasiness began to overtake me. I had come so far and waited so many years and yet now it seemed once more as if all my hopes had been misplaced. I gritted my teeth and made a private vow: this truly would be the last time I would ever allow myself to believe that there could be alternatives to the ever-turning cogs of the modern world. From this day forth I would put my head down and toe the line. If I didn't like the way the world was going that was my fault and no one else's: there could be no other way.

Half-way up the street I recognized the track by which I had entered the village all those years ago. I peered into the cool shade of the wood: the track was still in use. That much was for sure. There were fresh hoof marks and cart rucks. But then nothing could be read into that. The track led to other places too, not just the farm.

I adjusted my backpack and looked around. Down the street, past the side of one of the houses, I could see an old villager fitting a bridle to a horse. I took a deep breath and made my way over to him. The villager stopped what he was doing and looked at me whilst with one hand he calmed the horse by stroking its mane.

I greeted him in Japanese. His response seemed friendly enough, though I couldn't understand his rural dialect. My Japanese was very rusty and I tried in several different ways to ask him about the farmer but he simply grinned back at me and shook his head in incomprehension.

Finally, I delved into my bag and found a pen and a piece of paper and, working as carefully as I could, I wrote out the Japanese characters that spelt the farmer's name: Takeshi Fumimoto. A look of instant recognition lit up the old man's face and he immediately pointed back towards the track through the wood and muttered something that I couldn't understand and then slapped his hand on his horse's flank and made a gesture that seemed to suggest that he would take me there. He continued to chatter in dialect whilst he finished the job of readying his horse, and then when everything was prepared he motioned for me to climb up onto the cart. I hauled myself onto the single wooden plank that was the seat and slung my backpack into the empty cart. The old villager climbed aboard and with a twitch of the reins we were underway.

What this all meant I did not know. I had already spent so much time speculating about the fate of the farm that I was not going to spend another second trying to read anything into the gestures and actions of the old villager. He had recognized the name of the farmer and that was all. It didn't mean that the farm was still there, it didn't mean that the old stone farmhouse was anything other than a derelict ruin, and it certainly didn't mean that the farmer was living a happy life married to his true love.

Perched on the hard wooden seat, bouncing along the uneven track through the cool wood, with the old villager occasionally muttering something to himself, I tried to relax and put myself into a state of mind where I would be indifferent, no matter what I was about to discover.

B ut as the cart made its final turn over the brow of the wooded hill I was left speechless with amazement.

Before us on the road, two children were playing, skipping like lambs, back and forth through the farmyard gate. I was so astonished by this unexpected sight that all I could do was stare at them as if they were unicorns.

But when I noticed in the distance that there were three young men walking back from the fields below the house and two further people in the orchard to our right, my astonishment turned to wonder. I spun my head this way and that and saw other figures hard at work on the slopes of the orchard. Five, ten, fifteen people, men and women, young and old, more than I could count. I scanned the far slopes of the hillside, searching for the barren land where all those years ago I had passed the morning, scythe in hand, but all I could see were luscious orchards. I hunted in the fields to the north, expecting to see the black lands where the harvest had failed, but all I saw were swathes of golden rice plants rocking gently in the summer sun.

The farm had been reborn and everywhere I looked nature was in full bloom, everywhere there were people working in the fields and from the chimney of the farmhouse a column of smoke rose into the still morning air. More than any flag could be, it was a declaration of habitation and life.

The villager touched the reins and the cart drew to a halt just up the track from the farmyard gate. The old man pointed ahead with outstretched arm and nodded.

"Fumimoto-san."

I transferred my gaze from the riot of nature all around me to the farmyard. There I saw for the first time in seven long years my friend the farmer. He was as busy as ever, stooped over a box of freshly picked fruit, sorting it into different sizes. My heart filled with joy and I leapt from the cart, forgetting even to grab my backpack, and bounded down the track.

As I entered the farmyard, the two children began to chatter and laugh. They scampered over to the farmer's side and tugged his clothes. He looked up from his work to see what all the fuss was about. He had not changed at all. He looked just as youthful and vigorous as when I had first set eyes on him all those years ago.

When he saw me his face lit up in an enormous smile. He wiped his hands on his shirt and without hesitating for even a second he walked straight over. We met in the middle of the farmyard and embraced.

"James! I have been expecting you. I knew you would come …"

I was so overwhelmed by emotion that at first all I could do was shake my head and smile until eventually I managed to muster a few words.

"I am so glad to see you. I am so happy that it has all worked. I can hardly believe my eyes."

The farmer clasped me by the arm.

"And I am glad you have returned. At last I can show you the fruits of your labour! But come. First, I must show Masumi what I have found!"

"Masumi is here?"

The farmer smiled and turned to the children and speaking gently in English he said: "Children, where is your mother?"

Then he spoke to them in Japanese and at once they scampered across the yard and disappeared through the door of the farmhouse. He turned back to me.

"The barley harvest was successful. We married in the spring the year after you left. The little boy is called Akira and the little girl is called Aiko."

I stood speechless in the middle of the farmyard scarcely able to take on board all that was happening. The farmer took me gently by the arm.

"Come. Let us drink some tea together, and then I will show you the farm. It has changed since you last worked here!"

Shaking my head in wonder I walked beside him to the door of the farmhouse.

"But how did you know I was going to come?"

He paused for a moment with his hand on the door and turned to me and smiled.

"The spiders were here three days ago, for the first

time in seven years. I have been waiting for you since then."

Inside, the farmhouse had changed. It was set up so that many more people could sit around the hearth together and share their meals, and now that it was clearly used by so many people, it no longer had the austere atmosphere that it had when the farmer and I shared our meals together all those years ago.

Over by the fireplace stood Masumi. The two children were now hiding behind her legs. She was even more beautiful than I remembered. When she saw me she smiled and said something to the children in Japanese.

With a grin on his face the happy farmer spoke.

"Masumi, you remember my old friend. It is to him that we can give thanks, for seven years ago he worked with me in clearing the top orchard, which now has two thousand strong young saplings growing in its bounds, and enough vegetables to feed a small city ..."

Masumi smiled warmly and gestured to me to have a seat by the fire.

"Of course I remember James ..."

She turned to address me in her soft voice.

"Takeshi has been hoping for so long that you would come."

She poured me peach tea from the kettle that was still suspended from the fire and cleared away the lunch bowls from around the hearth, and then we all sat down together. The farmer sensed that I was overwhelmed by all that I saw and with great affection he gently teased me.

"James, you seem amazed to find us here today. You needn't have doubted so much! I told you we would make it ..."

I smiled at him and shook my head.

"I *am* amazed. Never in my wildest dreams did I expect to find all this. You have not only survived these seven years but you have created a new world. And I don't think I will ever be able to explain to you how happy I am to find that you are still here and that your new path has borne fruit."

The farmer grinned and shrugged his shoulders.

"We have a few more people. Some of the old farm workers came back and then some workers joined us from other farms. They prefer the way things are done here. And then there are the students who come from Yokohama and even from Tokyo to learn the natural way."

Masumi smiled and raised her beautiful eyes to look me fully in the face.

"And we have five children living here as well as all the young people from the universities. The children play in the fields and help with the work, and have the perfect childhood."

The farmer spoke again. He could no longer hide his pride.

"And Pilgrim, do you remember when we walked down into the fields and I said that one day my natural rice plants would rival the productivity of the commercial farms? Well, this year we will yield twenty-three bushels per acre in the bottom field, which is more than anyone has yielded in the whole of Ehime, which means, almost certainly, that these fields are the most productive in all of Japan!"

I could hardly believe my ears. But I had to know the truth.

"So you never gave up? You never cracked. You have never used pesticides or fertilizer?"

"Not one single drop!"

"And you have still never ploughed?"

The farmer shook his head and smiled. Truly, what had been achieved here by this humble man was a miracle worthy of God himself.

For the next three hours we talked. I told them of my new life as a teacher and I listened as the farmer and Masumi recounted their story of the last seven years.

It had not all been easy. Far from it. Even after the successful barley harvest, which had meant that they could finally marry, they had still suffered many terrible setbacks.

In the first year after their marriage, the neighbours on the huge commercial farms that surrounded them on all sides got together and attempted to sue the farmer, saying that his fields and orchards were the breeding grounds of all kinds of pests and that these pests used the farm as a base from which to attack their own healthy crops. They took the farmer to court in Ehime Capital and told the Judge that the Fumimoto farm was a vermin-infested wilderness.

The Judge came down in person to inspect the land. He was a very severe-looking man and when he first stepped out of his chauffeur-driven car he seemed most unhappy at having been made to travel so far into the countryside. But as soon as he got out into the fields his whole manner changed and he spent the afternoon sitting in the orchard in the sunshine, with his eyes shut and a smile on his face, surrounded by wildlife.

He returned to the provincial capital and the next day he threw the case out of court, saying to the commercial farmers: "If you do not like the way Fumimoto-san farms then take your case to God. I will have no part in prosecuting such a paradise."

In the second year, they had continued to lose many more trees and at one point things had looked very bleak. The farmer admitted that in those dark days he had experienced, for the first and only time in his life, the treacherous stirrings of doubt.

But with Masumi's encouragement he had persevered and by the third year of their marriage the farm was thriving and everyone in the Prefecture had heard of its fabulous success and the mysterious method of "do-nothing" farming. Workers from other farms began to ask to join them and students started to travel from far and wide to find out more about the new way to live their lives.

Success inevitably led to fame and fame led to outside interest, even from the very authorities who had always sneered at the farmer's techniques. In the summer of the fourth year the farm received a visit from the Ehime Agricultural Institute. An entire delegation came. They brought all sorts of apparatus with them and squatted in the fields, measuring the strength of the sunlight and the angle of the leaves and taking soil samples back to their laboratory so that they could establish the acidity or alkalinity of the earth. They wandered this way and that through the rice plants and the orchards, scratching their heads and looking positively annoyed. Some of them were carrying big nets to catch insects, others had small briefcases filled with phials of chemical solutions. All of them were dressed in white lab coats and all of them wore dark frowns.

"Are you sure you haven't been using fertilizer?" they asked the farmer suspiciously. "Are you absolutely certain that there have been no pesticides sprayed? Something strange is going on ... We are not getting the whole picture."

They spent two more days conducting experiments. One of the young students from Tokyo said it was as if a supernatural phenomenon had been reported on the farm and that the scientists were determined to find a "logical, scientific" explanation to replace the "superstitious" belief in nature.

Eventually, they packed up and moved on, unwilling to admit defeat but managing at least a grudging respect for the farmer's "good luck".

In the spring of the fifth year, just after the barley harvest, a man from Yokohama testing centre itself arrived. He had heard all about the "do nothing" method and he intended to grow rice using the technique, but he intended to do it under laboratory conditions. He began by marching into the fields and measuring the lengths of the straw that had been put back over the harvested field. Back in his laboratory, he announced, he would make sure all the straws were the same length and he would lay them in neat rows. The farmer smiled and chuckled to himself.

Finally, in the sixth year, the mystery as to who owned the land on the hillside was solved. It all belonged to a wealthy man, the descendant of one of the island's oldest samurai families. This old aristocrat had learned of what the farmer was doing and he came by horse to inspect the hillside for himself. He was a man of few words, as befitted someone of his station. He had taken one look at the marvellous orchard and immediately turned his horse for home, stopping only to tell the farmer that he would instruct his lawyer to give him not only the orchard but all the wild land up to the banks of the River Sumoda. "You know better than I how to care for our land," he said as he left.

As I listened to all these tales I was overcome with joy and hope. Here, all around me on the farm, was the living, growing proof that a new life was possible after all and that the path to this new life ran in exactly the opposite direction to the grey road of economic progress. The efforts of science were all unnecessary and only led to spiritual and physical hunger and pain. The evidence was incontrovertible. The farmer had systematically removed all the props of the modern world and yet his farm was now the most successful in the whole of Japan.

"Maybe now people can be persuaded to change. Maybe now they will realize that 'progress' is not just about more science and technology. Maybe others will even try your method!" I said.

"Non-method!" the farmer corrected me with a grin on his face. I couldn't help but laugh.

"Yes. Non-method!"

"Well, that is what I sincerely hope."

"Perhaps you could write an agricultural handbook – you know, like the handbook that the Ehime Agricultural Co-operative produces for the commercial farmers – only make it for natural farmers."

The farmer chuckled.

"Yes. And I can explain in long scientific phrases that the main technique of my non-method is 'to do nothing'!"

He guffawed merrily at this thought, then suddenly went quiet and put on a mock-serious face.

"My neighbours the commercial farmers are always saying 'What else can we do?' 'What else can we try?' 'Maybe we should try doing this or that?' They sit up at night dreaming up new schemes and worrying about what they might have forgotten to do. They read the literature sent to them by the Co-operative and tumble over one another to adopt the latest technologies."

Again, in an instant, his face lit up with a great big grin.

"I am the opposite. When I get up in the morning I say: 'What can I not do today? What else can I leave out? Shall I get up early this morning and put pesticides on my crops? Never! The natural predators will be my pesticide. I will have a lie-in. Fertilizer? No need! The straw and chicken manure provide plenty of organic nutrition. I'll take the afternoon off! Ploughing? Forget it! The worms and microbes will be my ploughmen, they plough for me day and night, even as I sleep they are hard at work …"

ater that afternoon, the farmer walked me through the fields and orchards and showed me where we had cut the weeds all those years before and where the dead fields used to be. Orchards of strong saplings and fields of healthy rice stood in their place. The natural balance of the land had been restored and nature's harmony had returned. Then we climbed the slope to the edge of the wood and sitting amongst the long grass we watched the sun setting over the fields below.

Half to himself, the farmer spoke.

"The only real natural farmer is the hunter and gatherer. Some happy people around the world still live like that. It is said that they only work a few hours a week and that they are never ill or unhappy. Diseases that are common here or in the West are completely unknown to them. Nature provides for them and they do not need to worry about planting schedules. That's the real natural farming!"

I played with a stalk of tall grass and meditated on his words for a few minutes. I thought of the crowds of London and all the other cities of the world.

"But we can't go back to that life. It is too late. There are too many people in the world and too many people who know nothing of nature ..."

The farmer studied the horizon and nodded his head.

"You are right ... But at least we can be on our guard against things that are called 'progress' but in the end only make us unhappy and unwell. The baboon in the forest – who is, after all, our cousin – is not always trying to improve his life and yet he knows how best to live.

When he feels a little unwell, he knows exactly where to turn to find the right herbs to fix his illness."

The farmer chuckled to himself and smiled at me.

"We can't even decide what to have for breakfast. Some people say we should eat no carbohydrates, others say we should eat no fat. Some say we should eat nothing but fruit whilst others say that meat and seeds are our natural diet. The truth is, we have forgotten, and we have forgotten because we have allowed our so-called intelligence to take over and we have lost our instincts."

The farmer smiled and shook his head.

"Every generation has its theory of nature. Once upon a time, people in the West believed that the whole universe was created by God in seven days. Today they say there was a big bang and that mankind has evolved from apes and before that from bacteria and before that from chemicals floating in the oceans of earth. They say that Einstein's Theory of Relativity explains everything and that Darwin tells us how we got here, but tomorrow it will all be gone and our view of nature will have changed again."

The farmer stood up and surveyed the horizon before looking down at me and smiling, his gentle, kind face bathed by the fading red glow of the setting sun.

"But nature does not change. Only we change. All our theories are just words and our words are not so different from the songs of the birds and the cries of the animals – except we make the mistake of thinking that our words contain the truth. But look! The first stars are out. Come. You must be hungry. This philosophizing is very tiring. I think we should stick to farming! Let us go and eat!"

I stayed for two wonderful weeks on the farm, sleeping in a hut on the mountainside, sharing meals with the farmer and his family and the student volunteers, and then finally the day came when I had to leave.

It was a far cry from the farewell of my first visit. At the hour of the mid-morning break, the farmer and his family and the farm workers and students all came back from the fields to say goodbye. I had worked with them all at one time or another over the course of my two-week stay and had shared much conversation and laughter, but it was the first time I had seen everyone together in one place, for at mealtimes people ate in shifts and drifted in and out of the main house, some choosing to sit in the garden and others preferring to eat in the fields. And so it was only now, just as I was on the point of leaving, that I was fully able to appreciate the measure of the transformation that had taken place.

I marvelled at the number of happy, healthy faces that I saw. Akira and Aiko, the farmer's little children, squealed with delight and played hide-and-seek between everyone's legs. There were ten, twenty, thirty, thirty-five people or more. One of the farm workers carried a tray out of the farmhouse piled high with deliciously sweet papaya fruit and we all gorged ourselves on this treat. Everyone was laughing and chatting: young and old, seasoned farmhands and novice students fresh from the city.

Then I noticed the farmer. He too was watching the gathering and he too seemed to be overcome by the sight of all the people. Perhaps he had never before seen everyone standing together in one place. It certainly wasn't his way to call big meetings. He taught by example, that was the only way he knew. I had never seen him call people to him, or demand everyone's attention. The most he would do was tap someone on the shoulder when they were on their own and offer a few quiet words of friendly advice.

As he surveyed the crowd of happy people I saw an expression of humble satisfaction cross his gentle face. Then suddenly his head turned. He must have felt my gaze. Our eyes met in recognition. Seven long years flashed by, from that day we had stood together in the top field, scythes in our hands, surveying the enormous labour that waited to be done, to this vibrant scene in the yard, everyone devouring the fruits of the farm, the laughing children, the sense of communal joy.

❀

The old villager from Fumimoto was waiting for me at the gate. His cart was laden with produce from the farm, destined for the markets and dinner tables of Ehime Prefecture. It was finally time to depart. I could delay no longer. The farmer made his way through the crowd and together we walked over to the cart.

"Now, old friend, I hope that it won't be another seven years before we see you again. And I hope this time you won't be worrying about us. As you can see, we have managed all right in your absence!"

I smiled and hugged the farmer to my breast and then turned and stepped up onto the cart. I shook my head and laughed.

"No. It's not you I worry about any more – it's the rest of the world. If only other people could see what you have done here then maybe they could be persuaded to change."

With his arm around his wife, the farmer joined the crowd in waving me off as the cart slowly rocked into motion and pulled up the gentle incline of the hill. Even today I can remember clearly the last words that the farmer shouted to me before he was lost for ever from my sight and even today, when I am feeling low, his words still echo in my ears and his strength comes down to me across the years.

"Have faith, Pilgrim! People can always change!"

EPILOGUE

EPILOGUE

Many years later, long after my second visit to Shikoku Island, I was driving through the Oxfordshire countryside when I passed a turn-off to an old abandoned farm. A newly painted sign had been erected that pointed down the drive and on it was some writing that included a large and conspicuous Japanese character.

I was intrigued. I had never before seen a single word of Japanese written anywhere in the English countryside. I pulled the car over a little way further down the road and then walked back up to the turn-off so that I could take a closer look. There, to my utter amazement, I read the following words:

"Do-nothing farming practised here. No plough. No pesticides. No chemicals. Come and try our tasty food!"

I could scarcely believe my eyes. I put my hand on the gate and looked up the track. It disappeared over the brow of the hill. Surely it couldn't be a coincidence? Although I had never been able to return to the farm in Fumimoto I still regularly exchanged letters with my dear friend the farmer and learnt with joy of his and his family's happy life, but he had never mentioned anything like this.

I breathed in decisively and pushed the gate open. I tramped along the gravel road for a few minutes until it took me over the hill and down into a collection of wooden farm buildings. I remembered these farm buildings from years before. I had passed them on several occasions on my long, weekend walks. But then they had been a collection of broken-down shacks, whereas now they appeared to be in complete working order and showed every sign of life. The roof of the farmhouse was new and the window frames and doors on all the buildings looked as though they had all just been freshly painted. Even the fences seemed to have been recently mended.

This was all very strange, for this part of Oxfordshire was no longer farming country, or rather the ever-expanding commercial operations had put an end to such small-scale farms.

I walked through the big iron gate into the farmyard, shutting it behind me, and when I saw chickens wandering free, pecking amongst the vegetable patch next to the main house, a smile of recognition began to cross my face.

Just then a young man came striding out of the barn. He looked surprised to see me. He had sandy-coloured hair and broad shoulders and he was dressed in jeans and a plaid shirt with rolled-up sleeves.

I spoke quickly.

"Hello! Sorry to bother you – I just wanted to see what your sign meant."

The young man smiled in return.

"It's no bother at all. We encourage visitors here. Please look around."

We talked and I told him that I was one of the teachers in the school not so far away. He knew the school. Some of his friends' children went there. As he spoke, I could not help looking around: could this young man really be practising the same farming methods as my old friend in Japan? Was it really conceivable that word had travelled this far – travelled in fact all the way round the world and right into my own back yard?

He offered to give me a quick tour and I accepted his offer readily. He clearly assumed that I would be deeply sceptical about his practices for as we went about the place he began to explain what he was doing, but he chose his words with great care, as if he expected me to be suspicious of these strange new ideas that so ran against the grain of modern life.

I asked him where he had learned his natural method. He replied that he had travelled to Japan and learnt it at the foot of a very wise man who had originated it there on his family farm. He clearly treasured his memories of this very wise man because when he talked about him he spoke in the most reverential way.

He then explained that, three years ago, he had brought back to England all he had learned and that now he had four other people working with him on the farm and they were entirely self-sufficient and the harvests were the best for miles around.

He led me proudly through the farmhouse and out onto the veranda that had a view of the fields down below. He talked to me about the pests and earthworms and about the ancient richness of the undisturbed soil. He was explaining the finer points of the natural method to me, but I couldn't hear him any more, I was staring in wonder at the fields before me and the tears were rolling down my cheeks. The young man noticed and abruptly stopped mid-sentence.

"Er, are you all right?"

I wiped my eyes and smiled.

"Yes. I'm sorry. It's a long story. I'm fine. In fact I am much better than fine. I think I'm the happiest I have ever been."

When I think today that the farmer, trusting only in his own judgement and courage, dared to follow his insight that mankind knows nothing and turned his back on all the supposed advances of the modern world, and by so doing transformed a barren hillside into the most successful farm in all Japan, I am convinced that human life does not have to be without meaning.

And when I remind myself of the humiliation that the farmer suffered at the hands of his neighbours, the setbacks that he endured at every turn, the risks that he took and the sacrifices that he made to bring about this transformation, I am overcome with awe for this simple farmer who trusted only that if he followed his heart, nature would reward his faith.

To the memory of
Masanobu Fukuoka 1913-2008